Lucky Star

Lucky in Love Series - Book 1

Anne Stone

Manchester Road Publishing

Lucky Star

Copyright © 2023 by Anne Stone

Manchester Road Publishing

The copying, scanning, uploading and distribution of this book, without the written consent from the author, is prohibited. If you would like to use material from the book (other than for review purposes), please contact the author.

This is a work of fiction. While the story takes place in the fictional town of Lucky, Ohio, there is a town called Luckey in Ohio that inspired the author. Names, characters, places, and incidents are the product of the author's imagination and are fictitious. Any resemblance to actual events, locales, or persons, living or dead, is coincidental.

All rights reserved.

Print Book ISBN: 979-8-9880584-0-3

Book Cover Design: RCMatthewsArtist

Edited: CEOEditor, Inc

For my Elizabeth

"You may be my lucky star.
But I'm the luckiest by far."
Madonna

Prologue

Las Vegas, NV

Chase Devine woke with a smile on his face.

He scratched his chest, and the sheet pulled away from his naked body. Hell, he couldn't see a damn thing. The room was still pitch dark.

A bright streak of sunlight slapped him in the face when he finally opened his eyes. Whoa. He squinted, then squeezing his eyes shut again, he gave his inebriated brain cells a time-out. Scenes from the night before trudged through his brain. Barhopping. Drinking and dancing. More drinking. Then sex—great, mind-blowing, off-the- charts sex.

His smile widened.

He rolled toward the woman lying beside him. The heat from her equally naked body drew him in like a moth to a flame. He reached across to glide his hand down her arm and opened his eyes for a second time. A gap in the curtains allowed the dazzling Nevada sunlight to shimmer on a familiar mass of auburn curls.

But why was it familiar? His muddled brain was slow, but finally, the identity of the person clicked.

Holy shit.

Megan Howard.

He whipped his hand back as he sat up far too fast, and his head exploded in pain. He massaged his temple as a combination of dizziness and nausea hit him. He flopped back down and closed his eyes and took a few deep breaths before covering his face with his pillow.

Every detail of their barhopping adventure came rushing back to him. Deep breaths... in and out, in and out. He repeated the mantra mentally.

Waking up next to a beautiful naked woman under any other circumstance wouldn't induce panic. But he was in bed with his best friend's younger sister. He was in holy deep shit without a shovel or a cross.

Finally, despite the hangover of the decade, rivaled only by his freshman year at State, he sat up. Edging over, he slowly swung his legs over the side of the bed. Securing his elbows on his thighs, he massaged his aching head.

She must have heard the pounding of his heart or the throbbing in his head because Megan stirred. Rolling over, she stretched, and the sheet pulled away.

Chase turned when he felt her movement but quickly averted his eyes and tucked the sheet gently around her, then scrubbed his hand over his stubbled face. How had he gotten here? Scratch that. He knew how he got here. The question was how was he going to fix it?

Hook-ups had never been his thing. He couldn't remember the last time he'd gotten shit-faced and screwed someone. Never. Shit-faced, of course. Screwed people, sure. Come on, he was thirty. But not like this. This type of thing didn't happen in Lucky. Small towns bred gossip.

A night of partying with a pretty stranger away from home was a whole other situation. Megan was no stranger. Things had gotten out of hand last night.

If the horny drunk bastard's shoe fits....

It had been reckless. Crazy. Stupid. As soon as Megan woke up, they'd discuss it like two adults and decide what to do.

He hadn't seen her in a year, maybe longer. She'd been away at school. And after her brother, Kell, had joined the Marines, there hadn't been a chance to get together. Not like when they were growing up and he'd been at the Howards' house every chance he got.

Anyplace was better than his house.

With eight years between Megan and her brother, it wasn't like the boys hung out with her. She'd always been the pesky little kid trying to tag along everywhere they went.

Had he been in the same circles, he might have noticed her mesmerizing green eyes or that she'd matured in all the right places.

Chase glanced over, studying her. Pinching the bridge of his nose, he tried to swallow, but his dry mouth made it difficult. Reaching across, he brushed a stray strand of her hair.

God, she's beautiful.

Sighing, he slipped out of the bed, heading to the bathroom.

He'd wake her up when he came out. No waffling. They needed to talk.

Chase washed his hands and splashed water on his face. He brushed his teeth, staring at his reflection. How was he going to explain this to Kell? He'd promised Kell he'd look out for his mom and little sister.

He'd broken his promise.

Truth be told, when Ruby Howard had asked Chase to go to Vegas to watch over Megan, he'd agreed. Ruby had said, "Make sure Megan didn't get into any trouble after the Songbird contest. Keep her away from strange men in bars."

Uh-huh. Right.

Looking back, he realized he'd readily agreed not only because he'd promised his best friend and it was the right thing to do, but also because Megan had caught his attention a few years back when she'd been home from college. Still too young, he'd ignored the attraction.

He never should have agreed, but Mrs. Howard could be very persuasive. She worried about her "baby." From what he'd seen last night, Megan could take care of herself. She was twenty-two years old, for God's sake. She was no baby. The change from little girl to adult had smacked him in the face. She'd rocked his world and charmed the pants right off him. Literally.

Megan stretched. Best. Dream. Ever. She kept her eyes closed, replaying the scenes in her mind. She didn't want to interrupt the crazy, hot sex she was having with Chase Devine.

She sighed and smiled.

Wow, did he live up to his name or what? How many years had she crushed on that man, wanting him to notice her? Only to be ignored by her big brother's best friend. What a sad cliché.

But in her dream, there was no such cliché. Nope, she held his undivided attention while he focused on every inch of her body.

The bed shifted.

Oh my God.

She realized two things in that instant: she was not alone, and it was a very real possibility her sex dream hadn't been a dream at all.

Squinting, she peeked at her surroundings. This wasn't her hotel room.

She slammed her eyes shut as a wave of nausea hit her. The sheet drifted down, and she realized something else.

She was naked.

Megan inched up, bracing her back against the headboard. She used one hand to hold the sheet in place and her other hand to cover her mouth to suppress the need to vomit. The toilet flushed, and she jumped.

The man from her dream emerged from the bathroom. He wasn't wearing any clothes. Not a stitch.

"Chase," she squealed, as she pulled the sheet up to cover her face. "So, I wasn't dreaming," she whispered. She'd spent the night with Chase. Megan wasn't sure if she should crawl under the bed or high-five herself.

The hell with crawling under the bed. This occasion deserved a happy dance.

But her mental celebratory dance tripped up as another wave of nausea slammed her. "I'm gonna be sick." She hauled, with no grace at all, her sheet-wrapped ass into the bathroom. She didn't realize Chase had followed her until she felt his cool touch on her neck and forehead. He pulled her long hair back and held her head as she paid her dues at the porcelain throne.

Great, you finally got Chase to pay attention to you. Barfing your brains out.

Embarrassment wedged its way in, ruining her happy moment.

"Shhh. You'll feel better in a few." He applied a cool washcloth to her forehead. "Can you hold on to this while I get you some water?" She nodded, then rested her head on the rim. Classy. Real classy. Seconds later, he tipped a cup of cool water to her lips. "Here, take a couple of sips."

She mumbled, "Thanks."

He'd donned a pair of shorts. "Think you can lie back down?"

"Yeah."

He helped her back to the bed. "Chase, did we"—she pointed back and forth between them— "sleep together?"

His eyes narrowed. "You don't remember last night?"

She shook her head. "No, it's all a bit fuzzy."

He frowned. "Well, from the number of condoms in the trash, I'm not sure there was much sleeping."

Heat flooded her cheeks. It was her turn to frown, but she refused to be embarrassed. They were consenting adults. Ignoring his comment, she shook her head. "I'm sorry. I'm playing catch-up. I've never drank that much. I remember some of last night—running into you in the bar after the disastrous contest."

Chase nodded. "Yeah. You were pretty upset. By that time, you'd started to drown your sorrows. We talked for a while and then took off on an impromptu bar crawl."

"I remember that. But it's everything afterward that's foggy."

Chase narrowed his eyes and frowned.

"What? Stop frowning at me. What's your problem?"

"Nothing." He turned away and shrugged. "It's just... well, I guess it's safe to assume the earth didn't shake, rattle, and roll for you? Apparently, I didn't rock your world." He laughed, but it sounded forced. Was it possible Chase was insecure?

"I'm not saying that. It's quite possible you did. I was having an awesome sex dream just before I woke up, so..."

"Yeah?" Now the corners of his mouth turned up. "It was pretty awesome." He grabbed a shirt from the floor and pulled it on over his head.

Megan took another sip of water, then set the glass on the bedside table. Rubbing her temples, she asked, "Remind me what you're doing in Las Vegas again. Besides this." She waved her hand between them.

His expression turned serious. He'd perfected that look years ago when she pushed her pestering too far. "Look, I'm sorry.

Things got way out of control last night. I mean, holy shit, you're Kell's baby sister."

She stiffened. Folding her arms across the sheet that draped her, she said, "I'm not *just* Kell's baby sister. I'm twenty-two." No way was she going to allow him to play the age difference card. And he was ignoring her question.

"I'm aware of that, and I also know when I was twenty-two, you were fourteen." He paced the length of the room. "Shit. What am I going to tell Kell?" He ran a hand through his hair. "I promised him I'd keep an eye on you. I'm pretty sure this wasn't what he had in mind. He's getting shot at in the Middle East, and here we are...."

Glaring, she scooted off the bed and grabbed the dress she'd worn last night. If they were going to have this argument, she'd rather not be wrapped in a sheet.

"Turn around."

"Really? Now you're going to be modest?"

"Really? Now you're going to be a jerk?" she mimicked.

He shook his head but turned his butt around.

Once in the dress, she was ready to take him on. Hands on her hips, she said, "First, no one is holding you to a promise you made when I was thirteen. I'm an adult."

He stopped pacing in mid-stride. He didn't respond for a beat or two. Finally, he turned and through gritted teeth said, "Kell is still my best friend. I don't think having sex with his little sister was what he had in mind."

Megan cringed and her stomach gurgled.

"Now you're being an ass." She took a deep breath and dipped her head. "Was it that awful?"

Damn him for making her feel insecure about herself. No way would she allow Chase or any other man that much sway over her self-confidence. "You know what? Whatever." She threw her hands up, then grabbed the rest of her clothes from the floor. She stomped into the bathroom and closed the door.

Her mental pep talk was fine, but it was Chase. She had years of romanticizing about him. There was no way she would cry in front of him. No way she would let him see he'd hurt her.

As much as she had hoped it could be different, she would always be the pain-in-the-ass little sister in Chase's eyes. Par for the effing course. No surprise. Nothing over the weekend had gone as Megan had hoped or planned.

Her single goal had been to win the Songbird contest. Winning would cement a gig singing backup for Nashville's iconic Sonny Dawson. But no, she placed second. Which was good, but not good enough. Sort of like being the second child and not quite as good as Kell.

Now, to throw gas on the flaming disaster of the contest, Chase was pushing her away.

Enough with the pity party.

She washed her face. Ran a hand through her tangled curls, then pulled it into a messy bun. She'd grab the rest of her stuff and get out of Chase's way.

His loss.

She'd head to Nashville anyway, because there was no way she was going back to Lucky, Ohio. She'd be smothered under her mother's overprotective eye and a small town full of busybodies. Lucky was a dead end. She refused to be trapped there like her mother.

Her phone buzzed.

It wasn't even eight o'clock, and she didn't recognize the number. "Hello."

So, this was how it felt to be an asshole.

Chase knew that was his guilty conscience talking. But he shouldn't make Megan feel bad about what happened last night. It was all on him.

The bathroom door swung open and hit the wall. She rushed out, stopping to pick up the rest of her things sprinkled on the floor. Her energy and excitement were tangible. What the hell happened in the bathroom? Was it his imagination, or had her mood done a one-eighty?

He cleared his throat. "Look, Megan—"

"Never mind, Chase. Don't worry about it."

He sighed. "Listen, I'm sorry. That was a shitty thing for me to say. I didn't mean it. It's just that this whole situation is... you must admit...."

His words hung in the air. It looked a lot like she was getting ready to bolt.

"Wait, are you leaving?" His head throbbed and his stomach felt like shit, but time was up—he had to come clean with her. He needed to fill her in on all that happened last night, since she had no recollection.

Shrugging, she said, "Don't worry about it. You were right. It was sex, nothing more. No biggie. Have you seen my other shoe?" She held up a single shoe.

He frowned. "It was actually a bit more." He didn't want her to leave thinking it had only been about sex.

She waved her arms and held up two shoes. "Found it."

She finally stood still.

"Look, I won't say a word to Kell. He'll never know. Yes, I'm leaving. You won't believe it, but I just got a call from Sonny Dawson's people."

Her voice went up an octave as she said *Sonny Dawson.*

"I don't understand. You didn't win the contest." He shook his head to clear his foggy brain.

"I know. But there was some screwup, so they want me after all."

"Megan, wait. What do you remember about last night?"

She stopped, turned. "I told you. After the fifth or sixth bar, the night gets blurry." Her eyes widened. "Wait. Please tell me we didn't have a kinky three-way with Elvis or something?" She raised her brows.

"What? No." He frowned. "Nothing like that."

She blew out an exaggerated sigh. "Oh, that's a relief."

He had to come clean.

Spit it out, Devine.

"Look, Chase. If our sex was as good as it was in my dream, then thank you. I'm only sorry I can't stick around for another round, because, whether you want to admit it or not, I'm a grown woman. Nothing to feel guilty over."

She pulled her phone from her pocket and studied the screen.

"I've gotta run. They're holding a cab for me. We have an afternoon flight to Nashville." Her excitement radiated in the room. "Oh my gosh, Chase, my dream is finally coming true. A singing career. And I'm going to be miles away from my mom and Lucky."

"Stop. Megan, please stop for just one minute. We need to talk. It's important."

"Next time I come home, we can hook up again." She winked. "But right now, I have to go. This is my big chance. What I've been wishing and hoping for since I was a little girl.

"You have no idea what it was like—" She took a deep breath. "I can't go back to Lucky. If I don't go now, I'm afraid I'll be stuck in that town for the rest of my life. This is my shot and I'm taking it."

How could he tell her now? How could he spoil this opportunity? He couldn't complicate her life. She looked so happy.

Chase happened to love Lucky. Except for his own parental nightmare, Lucky was home, the only place he ever wanted to live. But he could see where Megan was coming from. Her mom could be high-strung and a bit of a schemer.

Megan could never find out the real reason he'd come to Vegas. He'd fallen victim to Ruby Howard's manipulation himself.

Megan's phone rang, and she answered. "Yes. Sorry. I'm on my way down now. Uh-huh. Thanks." She faced Chase. "I've got to run. I still have to stop by my room and throw my stuff in a suitcase. Thanks for everything."

She turned at the door and skipped back over to him in the middle of the room. She leaned up, giving him a platonic kiss on his cheek. "Take care, Chase." Then she bustled out the door without a backward glance.

Talk about a wham, bam, thank you... sir.

He understood what it felt like to want something so bad everything else pales in comparison. Having an overbearing parent who tried to force you to comply to their will was something he could also relate to.

He moved to the tiny sitting area, where empty cans lined the floor. White Castle and Taco Bell bags littered the table. No wonder he felt like crap after a night of fast-food debauchery.

He shifted the trash out of the way until he found it. The undistinguished white envelope almost lost in the debris. No one would guess it hid a simple white slip of paper that had the power to change their fucking world. He pulled the sheet of paper from the envelope and stared. Tangible proof of their reckless night.

Sighing, he murmured, "Good luck, Mrs. Devine."

Chapter 1

Nearly two years later.
Nashville, Tennessee

The stage lights dimmed on the final note of "Honkytonk Angel," and Megan bowed her head. Applause exploded from the audience as she and her band took their final bows. As if they had rehearsed it a dozen times, which they had.

Smiling, she waved to her fans before she danced her way off stage, high on adrenaline.

Her assistant, Brenda Hines, handed her a water bottle with the lid already loosened.

Between gulps, Megan murmured, "Thanks."

Brenda had been her assistant for eight months. At only five foot three, what she lacked in height she made up for in speed and efficiency. Megan didn't know how she survived before Brenda came along. The woman was amazing. She seemed to know what Megan needed before Megan even realized she needed it.

Brenda was older by twelve years. Too young to be a mother figure. Which was a good thing. God help her if she had two mothers. The petite woman hit the sweet spot between big sister, BFF, and a very efficient right hand.

"Great show, Megan."

"You rocked."

"Awesome night."

Congratulations from the stage crew peppered her as she moved past the throng of people. These were the people who helped create the magic backstage every night.

She nodded. "Thanks, guys. I wouldn't be here without you all." She continued down the passageway to the dressing room.

"You have the quick interview with a reporter with *Nashville Tonight*. They were backstage filming from the wings—they want a couple of quick comments."

Megan nodded. "Thanks, Brenda." Waiting in her dressing room was a young woman she recognized from the local TV program.

Exhausted, Megan took a deep breath and mentally counted to three. Steeling herself, she smiled. The questions always got personal.

The pretty blond stood, extending her hand. "Ms. Howard, I'm Beth Young. Thank you for agreeing to this interview."

Megan shook her hand. Gesturing to the loveseat, she said, "Sure. Please sit and call me Megan." She took a seat across from the reporter. "Would you like something to drink? We have water and soft drinks in the little fridge." She nodded to the corner of the room.

"Water would be great, thank you."

Brenda stepped forward, handing the reporter a water bottle. Just one more reason Brenda was a gem.

Megan yanked off her heeled boots and kicked them out of the way. "So, Ms. Young, what is the feature about?"

"Please, call me Beth. We are highlighting some of the up-and-coming Nashville performers. With 'Honkytonk Angel' hitting the charts last week, we wanted to include you in the piece."

Megan smiled. She was flattered. "Honkytonk Angel" was her breakout song. Finally. It had been two long years since she arrived on the Nashville scene.

It felt like a million years since the Songbird contest, when she'd spent the night drowning her sorrow in booze, which had led to a night of unforgettable sex.

Wait, that wasn't accurate. She had forgotten. Or rather, she never remembered to begin with. The night was still a blur. But Chase still played a starring role in her most heated dreams.

"Is it true your career began after you won a singing contest in Vegas?"

"Yes. The prize was singing backup on Sonny Dawson's tour, and the rest, as they say, is history." Megan smiled at the reporter.

Megan had worked her butt off and paid her dues. Finally, with this song, she had a radio hit. It was getting play time on country radio all over America, and she was grateful. She still had a long way to go, but dipping her big toe into the Nashville pool of stars was exciting. Meeting her favorite performers, like Tim and Faith, Miranda and Luke Bryan never got old.

But with the fame came some negatives, too. Like obsessive fans. She didn't like to think about the odd shit that had been happening lately.

"How do you feel about the rumors that you're on the shortlist to be nominated for the CMA New Artist?"

"Of course, I'm excited. It would be such an honor. But the nominations won't be announced until the fall. I still pinch myself occasionally to make sure it's real." She laughed.

"Do you enjoy living in Nashville? Aren't you from a small town up north?" the reporter asked.

Megan stiffened but kept her smile intact. "Yes, I love Nashville. It's such a vibrant city."

"Where's your hometown?" the reporter reiterated her question.

Damn reporters. But it wasn't like it was a secret. She nodded. "A very small town in Ohio."

"What do you attribute for your jump to Nashville stardom?"

"It's all relative. But I've been here for two years. I guess if you want something bad enough, you work hard until it happens. I've gotten support from so many talented people on my team. Also, I'll always be grateful to Sonny Dawson. I've learned so much from him."

Ms. Young nodded, looking down at her notes. "What does the future look like to you? Marriage? Kids?"

Megan choked on her sip of water, and blinked. "I'm only twenty-four. My singing career is my only focus. There's no time for anything else, in my mind." She shook her head. Then added, "Not that there's anything wrong with marriage."

Although she was thinking who would want to tie themselves down to someone? To pour your heart and soul into a marriage that wouldn't last seemed pointless.

Relax. This isn't about your parents.

Brenda interrupted the exchange. "I'm sorry, but Ms. Howard must get to a party. One more question and that will be all."

Thank God for Brenda.

Megan muddled her way through the next innocuous question. She didn't have time to worry about the bizarre marriage question. Being a trouper, she'd do what she needed to do to get through the rest of her evening: party on.

Lucky, Ohio

Chase's duties as a firefighter varied. Some he enjoyed, some were routine, and some were downright dangerous. KP duty was just recently added to his list.

He finished the last of the pots and pans. Washed, dried, and stowed until the tedious process started over again in the morning. It wasn't the cleanup he minded. The company had always cleaned up after the meal. It was a mundane chore to help their feisty septuagenarian cook, Charlene Morgan.

The woman had been keeping the firefighters of Lucky well fed since before Chase was born. Keeping the small kitchen clean and neat was a small price to pay for that woman's beef Stroganoff. No, it was thinking of meals and then cooking them that he hated. He missed Char.

Tom, Char's husband, had had a stroke a week ago, and while his prognosis was optimistic, it meant Char was off until further notice. After Tom was released from the hospital and home from rehab, then they would assess her return to work. In the meantime, the men were taking turns cooking.

A cocky probie, Ryan Michaels, walked into the kitchen. "Hey, Cap, what's on the menu for tomorrow?" The probie did nothing to hide the shitty smirk on his young face.

Chase's eyes narrowed as he dried his hands on the dish towel. "I commend your interest. Since you asked, I'm going to reward you for being so conscientious. Your name just moved to the top of the rotation." Chase knew his response hit its mark by the look on the young man's face.

He squinted at the men sitting around the TV. "Don't you guys have your own duties to get to?" The group jumped up and dispersed.

"Hey, turn off the TV," he muttered. Damn, raised in a barn. He chuckled. There was something to be said for the mundane work. It helped Chase keep his mind off his personal problems.

Too much idle time and he found himself thinking about Megan. Daydreaming would be a better description.

But avoiding thoughts of Megan proved to be a challenge. It was difficult since anytime he heard her song on the radio, he was transported back to that weekend in Las Vegas. Without warning, he'd get the occasional text from her, which he replied to with far too much zeal for his peace of mind.

Could he ever get on with his life? Of course not, his common sense told him. Until she knows the truth about their night, he'd be stuck in the past. It was only a matter of time before he would come clean. He just needed to figure out the best way. Certainly not over the phone or in a text.

His parents weren't easy to deal with either, between his dad's badgering and his mom's cool indifference. His dad had a one-track mind. He wanted Chase to give up firefighting and join the family construction company.

Speak of the devil.

"Hey, what are you doing here?" Chase sprayed the antibacterial cleaner on the countertop and wiped.

"I'm here about my invitation. I want to know if you've decided."

"Invitation? Is that what we are calling it. More like a command."

His dad frowned.

"I told you I had to work. I'll be working a forty- eight-hour shift right in the middle of the meeting."

Dad's deepening frown showed his level of frustration. "Chase, look— "

"No, Dad, you look. We've been over and over this. I'm sorry Conner is gone. But that doesn't mean I'll fill his shoes. Devine & Sons Construction will have to get by without a son. Maybe it's time you changed the name."

Dad had worked beside Grandpa Devine from the beginning. When his grandpa retired, Dad stepped up to run the organization. After Chase's brother, Connor, died, it was Chase's turn to do the stepping up, but he had no intention of doing so.

Another day, another guilt trip.

"You're being unreasonable."

"No, I'm not. I have a good job, a job I love doing. You aren't going to take that away from me."

Dad's angry glare leveled Chase before the man stomped out of the fire station.

Chase didn't hate construction—he just loved firefighting more. He was willing to compromise, but so far, Dad had taken an all-or-nothing approach. His mom was a whole other issue.

Chase stowed the cleaner under the sink. "Hey, Captain, I wanted you to know I was kidding earlier. I didn't mean any disrespect," Ryan said. Chase smiled. Ryan was a capable young man and a damn good firefighter. No need to make him think he was in the doghouse.

"I know, Michaels."

Ryan sighed, relief all over his face.

"But you still have the morning rotation," Chase said.

"Yes, sir." Ryan grinned. "I'll get back to checking my turnout gear."

Chase nodded. "Good idea."

Nashville

"Thanks for bringing me home," Megan said through clenched teeth. *Relax.* She kept her hands busy fumbling in her purse as she dug out her keys. Without pockets, there was no other way to keep her hands out of Jason Sykes's reach.

He'd tried to hold her hand. Nope. This wasn't a date.

"You're welcome." Standing in front of the door to her apartment building, he added, "So, how about lunch tomorrow? I know a great place." His puppy dog eyes begged.

"Uh," Megan hesitated. She had been duped tonight. He'd told her a bunch of people were meeting up at the new pub down the street from the recording studio to grab a bite.

He'd offered to drive, suggesting that it would save her the hassle of trying to find a parking spot downtown. Usually that wouldn't have persuaded her. She liked to drive herself. But her car was in the shop for an oil change and tire rotation. So, she accepted.

She realized after twenty minutes no one else was coming. She'd spoken to him only a few times in the six months since he'd taken the IT job. He was a work friend—if she could even call him that. Still, he worked at the studio, so she played nice and went along with it. But only so far. One drink then she feigned a headache.

This was not cool.

"I'm sorry. I can't. I have plans."

"With whom?"

Whoa. None of your business.

Amazing how fast his eyes turned from innocent puppy dog to a scary pit bull. She frowned and took a tiny step away from him. Unfortunately, he was blocking her entry into the building.

What was wrong with some men? Why couldn't they take subtle hints? Why did they put women in the uncomfortable position of hurting their feelings? She simply wasn't interested in him in that way. End of story.

Megan shook her head. "Look, Jason—"

"Um, sorry. It's none of my business." He cleared his throat. "I just meant ... well, it doesn't matter. We can grab dinner instead."

Megan frowned. "Jason, I must be honest with you. I need to focus all my free time on my career. I'm glad we're friends, but anything else, if that's what you're looking for, isn't going to happen."

"I get it. But—"

She put her hand up. "My boyfriend and I just got engaged," she blurted—and immediately regretted it. She closed her eyes and inhaled. Damn him for pushing. Damn him for unnerving her.

His eyes narrowed. "Engaged? Since when? I haven't seen anyone around. I thought your manager kept a tight rein on you."

She stiffened. *A tight rein, my ass.* Megan cleared her throat. "He's from back home, and it just happened." Chase wouldn't mind. Would he? Besides, her heart belonged to him whether he knew it or not. Even after almost two years, the man still entertained her dreams.

"We haven't told anyone, so please..."

She kept digging the hole deeper.

Jason froze, standing eerily still except for his hands, which he clenched and unclenched. His stare freaked her out. She twisted her hands, wanting to flee into the apartment building and barricade the door.

"That's okay. But you have to eat, right?"

Swallowing her groan, she produced a fake smile. Anxiety, frustration, and anger raged within her. Sighing, she just wanted to get away from him. "Sure. As friends."

He grinned.

"Um, thanks. I really need to get upstairs. I'm expecting a call from my mom," she lied. Before she knew what was happening, Jason leaned into her and gave her an awkward hug.

Did he just sniff my hair? Ew.

Finally, she pushed free before he tried to stick his tongue down her throat.

Her hand trembled as she put her key into the lock and, stumbling into her apartment, she slammed the door. Then deadbolted it for good measure. As she leaned against the locked door, a shiver went down her body.

Emmie, her feisty little gray cat, greeted her as usual. Megan scooped her up and buried her face in the cat's soft fur.

All Megan wanted to do was take a shower. One thing was certain: she'd learned to listen to her intuition. And right now, her intuition was shouting "Beware."

Chapter 2

Nashville

The next day, Megan ignored the phone calls and text messages from Jason.

In the early afternoon, she made her an obligatory weekly call to Mom and immediately regretted telling her about Jason. Mom fixated on the idea that he could be boyfriend material.

Never.

Mom believed everyone should be in love. Sure enough, she mentioned the topic of grandchildren, and Megan ended the call with a quick "love you, Mom, gotta run."

She ordered a pizza and threw on a pair of comfy jogger pants and a Vanderbilt T-shirt, made herself a cup of tea, grabbed her Kindle, and snuggled into her favorite oversized chair. Emmie snuggled between Megan's thigh and the arm of the chair.

She'd always wanted a cat as a child, but Mom's dangerous allergy meant cats were a no-go. But when a friend brought a basket of kittens into the studio and Megan laid eyes on the gray, green-eyed beauty, she was smitten by her tiny meows. As if the kitten were calling to her, "Pick me. Pick me." So, she had. She chose the name Emerald—Emmie for short.

The intercom buzzed, and she hopped up, her mouthwatering in anticipation of the pepperoni and extra cheese toppings. "I'll be right back, sweetie."

She pressed the talk/listen button. "Hi, Megan."

It wasn't the pizza guy.

Goose bumps popped up on her arms. Through a clenched jaw, she said, "Jason? What are you doing here?"

"I stopped by to check on you. You haven't answered any of my calls or texts. We had a lunch date, remember?"

Shit. No, we didn't.

"Jason, I'm so sorry. I've been in bed all day. It might have been something I ate yesterday, or the flu and I have a terrible headache."

He ignored her. "I brought Chinese takeout."

Megan groaned. "Jason, that was kind, but food sounds awful. I can't eat anything but saltines and ginger ale." The lies flowed without a thought.

"Oh."

The silence between them was beyond awkward. Finally, she said, "Thank you, Jason. It was kind, but you should have called before coming over."

"I tried. You didn't answer your phone." His frustration was clear in his tone.

Oh, right. This guy would not take gentle hints.

"Look, Jason, I've tried to be kind. But you're making me uncomfortable. I'm not interested in anything beyond workplace friendship with you. I'm engaged, remember?"

She hoped the silence on the other end meant he had heard her and would now back off.

"So, I'll see you around."

"Yep. You will." The intercom went dead. What the hell did that mean? What an asshole.

At that moment, her cell phone rang. It wasn't a number she recognized.

This was the last effing straw. Why should she feel bad for standing up for herself?

"Listen, you need to back off," she shouted into the phone.

"Back off? What's going on, Megan?" Her brother's strong, concerned voice was so familiar.

Relief flowed through her. "Kell." She relaxed. Until she remembered, Kell rarely called. "What's wrong? Why are you calling? Are you hurt? I didn't recognize the number. Where are you?"

"Can't a big brother call to check in?" he asked. They had always been close despite their eight-year age difference. Silly of her to think it was anything but a coincidence that he felt the urge to check on her this afternoon.

"So, who needs to back off? Are you okay?"

"I'm fine. It's just some guy I work with."

"Are you sure you couldn't throw the poor guy a bone? I mean, after all, you are Megan Howard, Nashville's rising star." He chuckled.

"Ha, ha." She smiled. "I sort of did. Last night. And I'm not throwing him another. I told him as much, but I guess he didn't get the message. He called four times and sent ten text messages today. I ignored them all. Bad vibes, I guess."

She sighed. "Anyway, he came over here with Chinese takeout. I sent him away. I thought it was him calling again. I can't say why, but the guy gives me the creeps. He's pushy. Doesn't seem to understand I'm not interested. There was something strange—"

"Strange?" The light teasing was gone, replaced by the serious Marine. "What do you mean *strange*? Do I need to kick his ass?"

"No, calm down. I don't know how to describe it exactly." Kell had been a Marine for twelve years, so she understood his concern, but he needed to worry about himself.

"Try." She began to pace. "First of all, he tricked me into going out last night. He said there was going to be a bunch of people we work with, only when we got to the pub, no one else was there. No one else showed up.

"Then he blocked the door so I couldn't get inside my apartment building. He gave me a strange hug. I think he would have tried to kiss me. Crap, it wasn't a date. So that flat-out pissed me off."

"I'm calling Chase," he growled.

"What." Her voice skipped a few octaves. She stopped at her dining table and pounded her fist. "You will not call anyone. Especially not Chase."

"I don't like what's going on. He can be my eyes and ears."

"Oh my God. Kell, I'm a grown woman. I can take care of myself. I don't need you or anyone else rescuing me. And you don't need to involve Chase. It was bad enough you did that when you left home. Do you know how humiliating it was?"

"Too bad."

"You're exasperating. Besides, Chase lives like five hundred freakin' miles away. His eyes and ears won't do you much good. He has a job and a life." She'd die before she'd allow Kell to call Chase. When she saw Chase again, it would be on her terms.

"Damn it, stop being a stubborn ass. You must have gotten that from Mom."

"Watch it, bro." She could let the *stubborn ass* go, but comparing her to their mom was not cool. A silence fell between them. Megan tucked her hair behind her ears and went back to her chair beside Emmie.

Finally, Kell said, "It's hard being this far away. I worry about you and Mom."

"I know," she whispered. Actually, she didn't. She had no idea what it must be like for him. Sure, she was miles from home. But she could visit home anytime she wanted. If there was a crisis, she could be there in a couple of hours. Whereas Uncle Sam kept Kell on a very short leash.

"The world is full of hate and violence. It's an ugly place." He sounded sad. More so than usual.

"Oh, Kell. I'm sorry. I don't want to add to your stress. Please don't worry. You taught me how to protect myself, right?" She could hear shouting in the background. "Right, Kell?"

"Sure. I've got to go. Shit's happening. Watch your back, sis."

"I will. You be safe." She rushed to say, "I love you, Kell."

"Love you too, sis."

Chapter 3

Nashville

Jason slammed the bags of Chinese food down on his kitchen counter. He headed straight to the spare bedroom he kept locked. Megan's room. He jammed the key into the lock and wrenched the door open.

He flipped on the light, then swept his arm across the top of the short bookcase that sat along the wall. The collection of souvenirs he'd snatched from Megan's apartment scattered to the floor. It included a fancy bra and panty set, a tube of pink lipstick, a hairbrush, and a bottle of Katy Perry perfume.

The perfume bottle shattered when it hit the wood floor.

"Now look what you made me do," he screamed.

Go ahead, blame the bitch. But we both know this is all your mess. You're such a loser. She didn't make you do anything.

He put his hands over his ears, refusing to listen to him.

He stared at the photo montage covering the wall. Not an inch of bare wall peeked through. He'd pieced the collection together over the last six months.

After Megan had announced her engagement last night, he'd been doubtful. When he'd gotten home, he waded through the facts he knew about her and tried to think of an explanation.

How could she be engaged? He'd put his IT expertise to good use researching the internet for everything about her. There was nothing about a man from her hometown. She had to be lying.

Of course she's lying. You repulsed her last night. And she couldn't get rid of you fast enough. Face it, loser.

He grabbed his desk chair and heaved it against the wall.

What difference does it make? She isn't interested in you. Why would you think you could have someone like Megan Howard?

"Shut up." He punched the side of his head, desperate to get rid of the annoying, evil voice.

She's like all the others. She won't love you. Even Mama didn't love you.

Jason shook his head. He wouldn't listen. Instead, he studied each photo. The photographs calmed him. He had pictures of her performing at various venues. He also had everyday shots of her out in Nashville.

His favorites were the more intimate screenshot images.

He couldn't get any good pictures of her through her fourth-floor windows. So posing as a cable repairman, he had accessed her apartment with ease on a day when she was out. He'd avoided her skittish cat and placed a hidden camera in her bedroom. He now watched her most private moments, snapping images he could then download and print.

He moved to his computer desk to watch Megan as she entered her bedroom. She held her phone to her ear, chatting away. She didn't look sick. More lies. Then she left the room. She'd be back soon enough. He righted the chair, sat, and waited.

He'd have to think of a proper punishment. But he would worry about that tomorrow, and he'd make her understand she belonged to him.

Why were women so difficult? Why couldn't Megan cooperate? Like he had, when Mama locked him in the dark, smelly closet. He'd cried only a little.

He sat there in front of his computer screen for hours. Mama always said patience was a virtue. He learned early in his life to be patient.

Finally, Megan returned. It was dark outside, so she flipped on the light. He said a silent thanks since it helped the viewing quality. Jason slouched in the chair and readied for the show.

She moved to her dresser and pulled out a T-shirt and shorts he knew she slept in. She stripped off her pants and top, then off came her bra and panties.

By the time she was in bed, he had calmed himself and had a new plan. Tomorrow he'd deliver a box of chocolates and flowers. She needed to know he forgave her for her disloyalty. Then he'd get busy searching for this so-called fiancé.

Because Megan was his.

Chapter 4

Lucky

Chase sat at one of the round dining tables with the weeks' worth of mandatory paperwork spread out in front of him. He couldn't focus. Earlier today Ruby had mentioned Megan was seeing some guy named Jason, confirmation that his time had run out.

He owed her the truth.

He could only hope she'd forgive him for not telling her the truth two years ago.

He'd harbored the hope that he had rocked her world as much as she had rocked his, but that was clearly delusional since she didn't even remember their night together.

She was a beautiful young woman. Of course, she would date. But he hadn't dated.

Right. Like that is a fair comparison. You know about the mar-riage. She doesn't.

Whether in name only or not, he was still married to Megan, and until that changed, he was off limits. Not that Sherry Sloan took his hints. That woman didn't understand subtle, and it had taken some fancy footwork to stay off her radar.

He sighed, realizing he was a selfish Neanderthal who wanted Megan all to himself.

He needed to focus. He had to get this work done today.

It wasn't long before Megan's song, "Honkytonk Angel," came across the air waves. He should turn it off.

Why torment himself? But he couldn't bring himself to do it; instead, he let the melodic voice engulf him. He closed his eyes and pictured her as he last saw her, happy and carefree.

Hearing her on the radio, he could almost convince himself that he'd made the right decision. According to a recent Google search, the song was climbing the charts and a possible CMA nomination was mentioned.

If she was involved with another man, it was time to come clean.

He'd man up. Hell, he ran into burning buildings— he could manage a conversation with Megan.

It was time.

Yeah, you said that already.

Nashville

Had she been too hasty in brushing off Kell's concern? But damn it, she hated asking for help and now things were out of control.

Jason showed up at odd times, bringing her gifts like chocolates, flowers, and odd little stuffed toys. Nothing she said sank in with him. It was as if he was purposely being obtuse.

The gifts alone were unsettling. But even worse, he knew her favorite chocolates and that she loved daisies. How was that possible?

Even though she refused to go out with him, he worked at the rehearsal studio. He was always lurking. She felt his stare.

You're on stage. Everyone is staring at you.

But even when she was at home, she couldn't shake the creepy feeling she was being watched, and paranoia had her on edge. She wasn't sleeping well, and she felt like she might be losing it, because she kept misplacing things.

She'd begun to keep track of the number of hang-ups from numbers she didn't recognize. It was up to thirty-five. But she couldn't blame all those calls on Jason, since the numbers were all different.

The following Monday, Megan dropped by the studio office to pick up the sheet music for a new song her manager wanted her to record. He'd been cultivating her career to mirror Carrie Underwood's and thought it would be a perfect song.

Megan wasn't certain that was the way to go. There was no way she could come close to living up to Carrie Underwood's wholesome image.

Abby Carpenter, a blond and bubbly young Reese Witherspoon look-alike, greeted her. "Megan, a package came for you yesterday afternoon. I'm sorry I got busy and forgot."

Megan waved off her apology. "No worries." Abby had to be at least eighteen, but she could pass for sweet sixteen. The starry-eyed intern had a rare naivete not found in the music industry.

Megan pointed to the box on the counter. "Is that it?"

"Yep."

Megan grinned as she grabbed the package and flipped it over to see who sent it. Her eyes narrowed. "That's strange."

"Hmm. What's strange?" Abby asked, glancing up from the paperwork on her desk.

"No return address on the box. Who sent it?" It couldn't be from Mom. Packages from her usually had heart stickers all over them.

"Maybe it's from a secret admirer. Open it."

Megan smiled. "I doubt that. But let's look." She sliced through the tape and opened the box to find a smaller box. She slipped the lid off and shrieked, dropping the box immediately. The shrill echoed in the small office.

Abby jumped out of her chair. "What? What's wrong?"

Megan couldn't speak. She held one hand over her heart and the other covered her mouth. "It's a…" she trailed off. Trying again, she pointed to the box. "It's a dead rat or some kind of rodent. I'm gonna be sick."

She threw her hand up to her mouth and ran down the hall to the bathroom. Afterward, she rinsed her mouth and drank some water. What the hell was going on? This couldn't be happening.

She returned to the office, avoiding the box on the floor where it landed.

"I'm so sorry, Megan. I called the cops. Here, sit." Abby pushed a chair over to her.

Brenda barreled into the room. "What happened? I heard a scream." Abby pointed to the box on the floor.

Brenda leaned over to get a peek. "Oh, disgusting. What kind of sicko would do such a thing?"

Breathe. Breathe.

Megan put her head down between her knees. "What did the cops say?"

"They're on the way."

It seemed like an hour, but it was actually less than ten minutes when two cops walked into the office. Their names didn't register—Megan's brain was mush.

The taller of the two men looked like he was in his mid-fifties, close to her mom's age. The shorter officer looked younger. He had a sweet face and kind eyes.

"Who was it delivered to?" Taller Cop asked.

Megan raised her hand. "That would be me. Lucky winner that I am." She tried a little humor, despite seeing nothing funny about the situation.

Younger Cop asked, "Can we get your name?"

Apparently, these two didn't follow country music. An occasional reality check never hurt.

She nodded. "I'm Megan Howard." He jotted it in his little notebook.

Abby piped up, "She sings 'Honkytonk Angel.' It made number twenty-three on the country music charts this week. I bet you've heard it on the radio."

Taller Cop nodded, a blank look on his face. But Younger Cop smiled. "My wife loves that song."

Megan returned the smile. "I'm glad."

Taller Cop took a pencil and poked the box. Flipped it. "It looks like there's no return address."

No shit, Sherlock. But she held her tongue. It wouldn't help to be rude or to point out the obvious.

He continued, "Do you have any idea who would send this to you? Any disgruntled fans, boyfriends, or"— he cleared his throat— "girlfriends?"

She shook her head. No was on the tip of her tongue. Then Jason popped his head around the doorjamb. "Everything all right? I thought I heard a scream."

Megan rolled her eyes. Great. Just great. Of course, Jason was close enough to hear her scream. How convenient.

Abby stood, hands on hips. "No, it's not all right. Some asshole sent Megan a dead rat." She grabbed his arm. "Let her talk to the cops. Come on, Jason."

He twisted away from Lisa's grasp. "If you need anything, you have my number."

Megan turned away, ignoring him.

"So, Miss, eh..." Taller Cop looked at his notes. "Miss Howard. Can you think of anyone who would send this to you?"

"Please, call me Megan. No. I don't think so..." Both officers leaned in, listening, waiting for her to continue.

"You don't sound convinced. Is there anything else you can tell us?" Taller Cop pressed.

"Um," Megan hemmed and hawed, as Mom was fond of saying.

"Has there been anything else out of the ordinary?" the Younger Cop nudged. "Anything odd?"

Brenda stepped forward. She squeezed Megan's hand. "It's okay. You need to tell them what's been going on."

Megan motioned for Brenda to close the door. Younger Cop got there first and obliged.

"There's been other stuff. I've tried to ignore it, though I'll admit I'm losing sleep." Brenda squeezed her shoulder. "I've gotten lots of hang-ups from blocked numbers. Then I started hearing someone breathing on the other end of the line. More recently, I've gotten threatening text messages."

Younger Cop asked, "How many are we talking about?"

"Dozens. I saved screenshots and recorded each on my phone." She entered her access code and opened the saved messages.

"Here." She held the phone out for them to see.

Taller Cop raised an eyebrow. "And you haven't reported these?"

She shook her head. "I figured it was part of being a celebrity of sorts. I can't imagine how big-time celebs manage this crap." She shrugged. "I guess I thought you couldn't do anything about it."

"Any other suspicious activities?" Younger Cop asked.

Megan shook her head. "I don't think so."

Brenda cleared her throat. The two cops looked at her. "Megan, you need to tell them about Jason. Tell them everything."

"If there's more, we need to hear it," Younger Cop said.

"It's just that I don't want to get him in trouble." The two cops exchanged a look.

"Why don't you tell us what else has been going on. Let us decide," Taller Cop said.

"Okay, here's the deal." She sighed. "That guy who poked his head in here"—she pointed to the door— "his name is Jason Sykes." She spelled the last name for them. "He's one of the IT guys here at the studio. Lately, he's been doing some things that have made me very uncomfortable. I don't believe any are illegal, though."

She pressed her hand to her thigh to stop her leg from bouncing. It was an embarrassing nervous habit that had resurfaced recently. Not surprising.

Once she calmed her leg, she told them everything that had happened with Jason over the previous weeks.

"And think about this situation." Brenda pointed to the box with the rat. "He showed up a few minutes after Megan opened the box. Said he heard *someone* scream. But the IT area is on the other side of the building and up a floor. I used to think things were coincidental, but I'm not so sure anymore. There's just been too many."

The cops explained that Megan could file a complaint, try to get a restraining order.

Megan took a deep breath.

She had no proof that he sent the dead rat. Was it worth the commotion she'd stir up in the studio and with the band if she filed a formal complaint?

Taller Cop asked, "Can we forward those messages?"

"Yeah, of course, if you think it'll help put a stop to all this."

"Can you get yourself a burner?"

She nodded. "I admit I'm getting more frightened by the day, and this totally freaked me out."

Taller Cop continued, "Have you spoken to anyone in HR? They may have policies for workplace harassment. Think about a formal complaint or a restraining order. If the situation escalates, don't hesitate to call." He pulled his card from his pocket and handed it to her.

He pointed to the box and the rat. "We'll take this, check for fingerprints, but I'll be honest: I doubt we'll find any."

"You need to be vigilant. Be aware of your surroundings at all times. Don't hesitate to call us." Younger Cop gave her a reassuring look.

After the cops left, Brenda announced, "I'm coming home with you. I'll sleep on your couch. I don't want you alone tonight. This whole thing is very strange and upsetting. We'll stop and buy wine, dinner, and an inexpensive temporary phone for you."

Megan didn't argue.

Chapter 5

Nashville

Jason disconnected the call he was on with the head of the IT department. The jerk had fired him over the phone. Didn't even have the guts to do it in person. Some BS about complaints from his coworkers.

He knew exactly who was responsible for getting him fired. "That bitch." Jason bellowed as he slammed his phone down on his desk.

The whole rat thing backfired. It should have worked. She was supposed to come to him for help. But, no, damn it. She'd gone to the cops. She'd be sorry. He'd teach her a lesson.

Yeah, sure. Big talk from a little man. Of course, she didn't come to you for help.

He stared at his computer screen. Searching for something on Megan that he could use against her. She'd been in Las Vegas before coming to Nashville. The Songbird contest or some other inane name. Maybe he could find something about that weekend.

Three hours later, the pizza he'd ordered was long gone, and he was just about to call it a night when he finally hit pay dirt. He dug up a marriage license between a Chase William Devine and a Megan Marie Howard, dated two years ago. The bride's date of birth matched. It was her.

Though he had a hard time believing what he was looking at. Even with the proof right there on his screen, it didn't make any sense. Why would she keep a marriage a secret?

What about her so-called engagement she'd thrown in his face? That wasn't likely to be true if she was already married. He tapped the keyboard in search of evidence of a divorce or annulment but didn't find anything. More lies. Sweet Megan Howard had a few secrets. So much for her perfect image.

He picked up a framed photo of her from his desk. "Damn," he muttered. "You belong to me. I just need to get you alone, without interruptions, to convince you."

But why? She's a bitch. She got you fired. She's not worth your trouble. She's a liar.

"Shut up. She is worth it. I love her."

Whatever you say. But she'll never love you.

He threw the frame against the wall, shattering the glass.

"Why do you always ruin everything? She's mine. She has to be mine."

She'll never be yours. She won't ever love you. Mama didn't love you, and Megan won't either.

"Don't say that."

Why? It's the truth. Are you going to cry?

"Stop. Stop. Stop." Jason hit his head with his palm. "I need a plan. I need to think. Shut up and leave me alone so I can think."

If her fans learned the truth about her shotgun wedding, her Goody Two-shoes image would be tarnished. She'd no longer be out of his reach. She'd need a friend to lean on.

He hit the print key.

He'd send this information to her manager. The man controlled every aspect of her career. He was the one pushing her wholesome image.

If you destroy her career, maybe she won't think she's too good for you.

Chapter 6

Nashville

"What the hell is this?" Rich Reynolds fisted a piece of paper, waving it in the air.

Megan took a step back. Her manager wasn't known for subtlety, but he'd never raised his voice to her. The man reminded her of the Jerry Maguire character. Sleek and always put together.

She batted at the sheet of paper as it came close to hitting her in the face. "Whoa. Calm down, Rich." He continued shaking the paper. "Will you please stop waving that in my face and let me look at whatever it is?"

He shoved the paper at her. Her eyes narrowed on the words at the top of the page: Marriage Certificate.

She shrugged. What could this have to do with her? "So? I guess this emergency meeting isn't about Jason Sykes. Or the dead rat or any of the other odd things happening in my life."

He ignored her questions and snatched the paper back before she could read more.

Through clenched teeth, he said, "It might've been nice to know about your marriage. How am I supposed to do my job if you keep secrets, especially like this one, from me?"

Her eyes widened and she scoffed. "What are you talking about? Married? Never. Her parents' marriage was a disaster. It'd soured her on the idea years ago.

She grabbed the paper from his hand again and scanned down the page to the names and signatures. Blinking, she tried to comprehend what she was reading. She didn't trust her legs to hold her up, so she plopped into one of his guest chairs.

It can't be. It makes no sense.

"Are you telling me that isn't your name and signature at the bottom?"

Megan couldn't stop shaking her head. She tried to speak, but her voice came out in a whisper. "This can't be real. It must be a fake. Add it to the list of bizarre shit in my life right now. Someone is playing a bad joke."

"Who the hell is Chase Devine? I don't know the name."

She ignored Rich's question. "No way. I would remember getting married," she said incredulously. "Unless ..."

Rich raised his brows. "Unless what?"

She took a closer look at the certificate. At the bottom were the signatures of two witnesses whose names she didn't recognize. Under their names was listed the Vegas chapel where the ceremony allegedly took place. The Chapel of Bliss. The date coincided with the Songbird contest.

Holy shit.

Thank God she was sitting. Her hand drifted to her side as dizziness forced her head down and the paper slipped to the floor. She gulped for air. Had she been so drunk that night that she blacked out the fact that she'd gotten married? How the hell could someone forget something like that?

Because the thought of marriage makes you break out in hives. And causes your damn leg to bounce as if you're on the horse spring rider at the kiddie park. Megan squeezed her knee to stop the involuntary movement.

This couldn't be real. Could it?

She would have had to have been drunk beyond reason. Oh God, it must be true. She didn't remember any part of that night. Why had they gotten married? It made no sense.

She needed to talk to Chase. Did he remember? He couldn't. If he had, why hadn't he told her? She thought back to that morning in the hotel room. Had he tried to tell her? She couldn't remember the entire conversation. She'd been too excited about the call from Sonny's people.

It took Megan a second to realize Rich had spoken. She lifted her head. "What? What do you want me to say? I'm as shocked as you are."

"Really? So, it's fake?"

"No, I didn't say that."

Rich folded his arms across his chest. "Perfect. Care to share with the class?"

She glared. "Look Rich, I don't appreciate the condescension. Chill. I'll tell you what I remember."

"Go ahead."

"Two years ago, when I was in Vegas for the Songbird contest I ran into a guy from my hometown. I forget why he was there—a conference or something. But we saw each other in the hotel bar. I was drinking my way into oblivion after I lost the contest. He helped."

Rich raised his brow. "He helped you with more than that, it seems."

Megan rolled her eyes.

"Are you telling me that you got drunk and then hitched in some tacky chapel and you don't remember any of it?"

She nodded. "I guess. What do you want me to say?"

Rich shook his head. "What I want is for you to tell me unequivocally that it isn't true. That there is no way my client, who I have been promoting as the next wholesome Carrie Underwood, would get drunk and marry a stranger."

Megan frowned. "Chase isn't a stranger."

He glared at her. "It just gets better and better. Never mind, what we need to do is figure out how we're going to spin this. I need to get our publicist on the phone, now. The image we have been building will crumble when people find this out. I'll look at the options, either an annulment or a quickie divorce."

The dizziness faded. There was a piece of the puzzle missing.

"Wait, how did you find out? Where did you get this?" She gestured to the paper.

"It came in this morning's mail." He held his hand up. "And before you ask, no there was no return address."

She shook her head. "That's no surprise. It still could be a prank. There have been a lot of strange things happening to me lately." Her explanation sounded lame to her ears, and Rich probably thought the same.

He didn't appear to be listening anyway. Rich already had his ear to his phone, tapping his pen on his desk as he waited for someone to answer.

"Rich, wait."

He looked up and set his phone down.

"I need to take a few days. This whole business with Sykes has me on edge. I hate having to look over my shoulder all the time. Now this. I need a break. I'm going back home, to Ohio, and while I'm there, I'll have a chat with Chase."

My husband?

Lucky

The fire department managed a variety of calls. Besides fires, they responded to medical emergencies and other rescues. So far, it was one of the busier days.

One grease fire over at Joe's Bar and Grill and a bad multi-car accident out on the highway consumed most of the morning. The afternoon was taken up with pulling a boy from a dried up well, rescuing a bunny, and helping Suzy Johnson get to Lucky General in time to deliver a six- pound, ten-ounce baby girl who, Chase predicted, would wrap her daddy around her tiny little finger. It wasn't even four o'clock.

Chase would rather be home on his patio, looking out at the lake as he sipped a beer with one hand and petted his golden lab, Brady, with his other. There was something relaxing about the water and a four-legged best friend.

But he couldn't do that, so instead he walked across the street to grab a coffee at Bea's Beanery, the one with the For Sale sign in the window. Too bad. Hopefully, whoever bought the place kept the eclectic charm. The bright, cheery colors made him smile even on the dreariest day.

While he waited for his coffee, his phone vibrated. He stepped to the side and answered, "Captain Devine."

There was a bellow of laughter on the other end. "Seriously? Captain Devine? What are you, a superhero now?"

Chase smiled. "Ha, ha. Yeah, I know. It's my name and rank. And hell if the cape fits... Kell, buddy, it's great to hear your voice. How're you doing?"

"Can't complain."

Chase chuckled. He knew his friend's off-the-cuff response wasn't that at all. He admired Kell's fortitude. He admired all the brave men and women over there fighting their asses off for their country.

"What's your sorry ass up to?" Kell asked.

Coffee in hand, Chase stepped outside and parked his butt on a bench along Main Street. He stretched his long legs in front of him and took in the town square. "Can't complain either. Keeping busy. But, hey, man, is everything okay?"

"You know, same shit, different day,"

"Yeah, I bet. I—" Chase swallowed down the emotion in his voice. He loved this man like a brother. "I'm glad you're alive and kicking."

"Listen, the love fest will have to wait. I've only got a few minutes, and I need a favor. A big one, buddy."

Chase straightened. "What's up?" He'd known Kell for most of his life—he recognized the urgency in his friend's voice.

"It's Megan."

Oh shit.

"What about Megan?"

"I'm concerned for her safety. But you know how stubborn that girl can be. She won't reach out for help. I suggested she call you, but she went ballistic."

She did?

Focus on the topic at hand.

"What's going on?"

"Megan has an overzealous admirer. She downplayed it, as usual."

"When did you talk to her?" Chase asked.

"A few weeks ago. Ended up out on maneuvers— this is the first chance I had to call you. When I talked to Megan, she acted like it was no big deal. She could take care of it. But I sensed something in her voice. The guy doesn't understand the word *no*."

"I can call her," Chase offered.

"Here's where the big favor comes in."

"I'm listening."

"I'm afraid if you call her, she'll blow you off like she blew me off. I was hoping you could make a quick trip down to Nashville. Get her to talk to you. Scout out the situation. I'll cover your gas or a plane ticket."

Chase didn't respond immediately, and Kell rushed on.

"Never mind. It's a lot to ask, and I'm probably overreacting. But it's hell being so far from home. I can't help her. Uncle Sam has my hands tied."

Chase didn't believe in signs, but this seemed like a basic one. *What's that shit called? Kismet?*

"When my shift ends at noon tomorrow, I'll have the next forty-eight hours off. I can make a quick trip down to see her. Whether she'll talk to me is a whole other matter."

Kell sighed. "Thanks, Chase. See if you can get the truth about this guy. Not the sugar-coated version she told me so I wouldn't worry. Assess the situation, see if we need to get the cops involved."

Cops? "You think it's gotten to that point?"

"I don't know, but I have a bad feeling about it. I'm not willing to take a chance that some asshole is taking advantage of my baby sister."

Chase swallowed. Before he could respond, there were mumbled voices in the background. Kell said, "Hey, I need to go. Thank you."

"Stay safe."

Chase pinched the bridge of his nose and closed his eyes.

"That's the plan. Gotta go. Later." The line went dead.

"Yeah right," Chase scoffed. "Some asshole, huh?" He wiped his sweaty hands on his pants. "You run into burning buildings for a living. Remember that," he muttered to his self.

Chapter 7

Lucky

The next morning, the fire trucks pulled back into the station after an early alarm. Bad house fire. No one was home, only the family pet, a beagle, who they could save because of the Pet Finder sticker in the front window. She'd be okay. Scared, but safe and alive.

Thankfully, no one lost their life or got hurt.

The beagle's tag identified her as Bailey. She'd ridden back to the station with them and would stay there until they could notify her family. In the truck, she'd curled up in Chase's lap. As much as he soothed her, she still shook.

Chase climbed down from his seat. "Hey, Ryan, can you grab a few towels? I'll make Miss Bailey here a makeshift bed until we can locate her family."

"Sure thing, Cap."

Once their four-legged visitor settled into her bed, Chase stowed his gear. He'd just yanked off his shirt and was headed toward the showers when he got a text from Megan.

His chest tightened. He'd felt less anxiety running into a burning building.

Megan: We need to talk.

Chase: Okay. Sure.

Scowling at his phone, he willed it to vibrate with another message, one that made sense. Was she reaching out for his help?

He hadn't had a minute to himself to check on flights to Nashville. It looked like he might be making a road trip to keep his promise to Kell.

Craving privacy, Chase reversed direction and walked to the back entrance of the building. He'd call her if she didn't text back soon. Head down, focused on his phone, he turned the corner.

Whoomph.

He barreled right into a female bulldozer whose auburn hair brushed past his face. He recognized the familiar scent of coconut.

His eyes widened. "Megan. What the fu—" He grabbed her elbow to steady her. While Megan's hand flew to her chest.

"Chase, you scared the hell out of me."

"Yeah, I know the feeling." He knew he hadn't conjured her up in his mind.

That was definitely a solid body he'd slammed into. "What are you doing here?" Then he came to his senses. "Sorry, did I hurt you?" He squeezed her arm to emphasize his question.

Guess the trip to Nashville is off.

He didn't want to let go of her. Her silky smooth skin took him back to the night they'd spent together. He'd loved trailing his fingers up her arm and down her back.

He stood back and looked her over to make sure he hadn't hurt her. He tilted his head, willing her to explain.

She took a step back, too. "I'm fine."

"Megan, what are you doing here?"

Soot had transferred from his sweaty body to her light pink top. He frowned. "Sorry, we just got back from a fire. I was on my way to the showers when I got your text. Nothing a bit of laundry detergent can't fix." Chase shrugged and grinned.

Megan brushed at her top. His fingers itched to help, but he didn't dare. Instead, he clenched his fists at his sides.

"Yes, I can see that." She sighed dramatically and crossed her arms over her chest. Great. She was digging in her heels. "Chase Devine, I need to speak with you. Now. It's important."

His grin widened. If she only knew how adorable she looked. *From her expression, I better keep that to myself, unless I wanna get slugged.*

"Okay, Megan Howard," he teased, placing the emphasis on her last name.

"Shh." She put her finger to her lips. "I'm keeping a low profile on this trip."

"Low profile? What does that mean exactly? Does Ruby know you came home?"

"I didn't come home. I came to speak with you." Her eyes drilled into him.

He put his hands up in surrender. "Shit, Megan. All right. Of course, we can talk."

His chest tightened. Had she remembered? Or was she here for a different reason? But if she was, why the anger? He could feel it vibrating off her.

Time's up.

"Tell you what, let me take a quick shower. Ten minutes. Why don't you take a stroll across the street? I bet there are a few new stores since the last time you were home, and there's the little park in the middle of the town square." He waved toward the big window and nodded in that direction.

She turned her head to look. Her frown deepened. He didn't think that was possible. "What part of low profile did you miss?"

"Christ. You can't be serious." She didn't move. "Guess you are. Okay, one sec." He jogged to his truck, reached in the open window, and grabbed his baseball cap off the dashboard. "Put this on to hide all that hair. With your sunglasses, I doubt anyone will recognize you."

She thought about it for what felt like a full minute.

"Fine. Ten minutes." She pointed to a bench across the street. "I'll be waiting right there for you."

He nodded. "Got it. See you in ten." He tapped his watch, then turned, heading to the showers, although it felt like the gallows.

☘

Megan checked her watch. Ten minutes. That gave her time to gather her thoughts. She'd caught the first available flight and rented a car. Other than the one stop in the ladies' room at the airport, she'd been traveling since five this morning.

As she adjusted her long hair under the ball cap, she regarded the view Chase had pointed out. Main Street. Looked like someone had given the town a much-needed facelift.

Two years was a long time.

No one forced you to stay away that long.

She shrugged off that uncomfortable thought. Yet no matter how many times she tried to convince herself that she had not run away from something but rather had run to something, she still felt like it was a lie.

There were small details that, when put together, added up to give Lucky a charming vibe. Driving into town, she'd been too preoccupied to notice, but now she could appreciate the beauty that was evident up and down Main Street.

Several recycled whiskey barrels strategically lined the sidewalks. Each barrel overflowed with bright red geraniums, petunias of every color, and yellow marigolds. Green vinca vine poured over the rims. Overflowing hanging baskets hung from lamp-posts, alternating with the American flag.

Her view landed on a familiar charming storefront with a red-and-white striped awning, Bea's Beanery. Beneath the windows, flower boxes exploded with more color. Round tables and chairs created the feel of a European café. Megan squinted. Was that a For Sale sign in the window?

Bea's Beanery held a special place in Megan's heart.

The dear woman who owned it had given Megan her first job when she was sixteen. Did Beatrice Small still run the place? The woman had seemed old eight years ago. Wouldn't she be retired by now? Too bad Megan wasn't in town for a social visit. Next time, she'd like to stop and say hello.

She wandered farther down the street, passing Big John's Sporting Goods where Kell and Chase bought their baseball equipment as boys. Across the street, Joe's Bar and Grill still stood on the corner. It looked like someone had recently given the old place a new coat of paint.

She smiled. Her girlfriends tried to order beer with their burgers a few times, but Joe always caught on. He kept a careful watch over his customers. And when a bunch of teenagers came in, he was on high alert.

She hated to admit it, but she found the town charming. She took a seat on a bench facing the square and before she knew it, Chase plopped down beside her. His hair was still damp and curled at his collar. He wore jeans and a navy Lucky Fire Department T-shirt, his golden tanned arms exposed for her viewing pleasure. His biceps flexed and rippled as he slid on his sunglasses.

Oh, dear God.

Even with the dirt, soot, and God only knew what, he had still looked like a damn movie star. But freshly showered, wow. Just wow. Megan's face heated and her body tingled. He resembled the actor who played Christian Grey, sans the business suits. But that didn't mean he behaved like the character. Or did he?

Focus.

No doubt about it: he looked every inch a hometown hero.

Damn the man. Why did he have to look so good? He was even better looking than in her dreams, and her dreams were pretty damn good. Her adolescent crush crowded her judgment, making it difficult to hold on to her hurt and anger.

"Hey, sorry." Chase glanced at his watch. "One minute late."

"That's okay. I was enjoying taking in the sights on Main Street. So much has changed. It has a nice vibe."

Chase cocked his head. "You hit your head in our collision? Are you feeling all right?"

She caught the wicked grin on his face.

"Ha. Very funny. Things change."

"Yes, they do. And it has. I'm surprised your mom hasn't kept you apprised. Maybe she figured you were too busy or not interested."

Was that censure she heard from him? Was he picking a fight?

Megan stood and straightened to her full five foot eight and still fell a head shorter than Chase. "Listen, I didn't come here to discuss Lucky." She narrowed her eyes. It was time to get to the point. "Is there somewhere private we can talk?"

"Sure. I would suggest meeting in a public place. But since that doesn't seem to be an option, do you want to go to my place?"

Megan thought for a moment. "On one condition." She held up a finger. "No alcohol." Chase raised a brow but nodded.

"Fine. Let's go," Megan said, already walking back to her car.

Chapter 8

Megan followed Chase in her rental—he'd built a home outside of town on Lucky Lake. At least one positive perk of a family-owned construction company.

The only perk.

He pulled into his garage, hopped out, and met her at her car.

"Can I get you anything to drink?" he asked once they were in the house.

A head tilt and her *get real* frown answered for her. He held his hands up in a peace offering. "I have pop but no diet in this house, sorry. And several juices." He opened the fridge. "Orange, cranberry and V-8. And I have water, of course. Filtered, there at the sink." He pointed. "If you prefer something hot, I can make coffee, no problem."

"Water is fine, thank—oh." Brady rushed to her side. A new visitor to sniff and investigate, and he did all that while his tail wagged a mile a minute.

"Oh, aren't you the sweetest thing?" She bent to Brady's level and scratched under his chin, patted his head, and cooed praise on the dog.

Lucky dog.

Still leaning down, she asked, "Who is this handsome guy?"

Shit, Brady was already smitten. His tail hadn't stopped wagging, and he stared up at Megan with such adoration that Chase chuckled.

"This is Brady." The dog lifted his head and looked to be smiling. "Brady, this is Megan. Megan, this is my best boy, Brady."

"Oh, Chase, what a beautiful dog." She turned her full attention to Brady. "You're a handsome boy, aren't you? Yes, you are."

Brady pranced around, showing off. He picked up his tennis ball and dropped it at her feet.

"Yeah, I agree. He's my best bud. Aren't you, boy?" He rustled Brady's coat. "But don't touch his tennis ball. It's full of dog drool—" But Megan had already picked up the ball.

He chuckled. Oh, the look on her face was priceless.

"You can wash the drool off in the sink."

As she washed, he got a glass down from the cabinet. "Ice?"

"Yes, please."

He filled her glass and grabbed a beer for himself. "I assume it's okay for me to indulge in a beer?"

She rolled her eyes. "Funny."

He smiled. "Okay, why don't we go into the other room? It's more comfortable than the kitchen."

She followed Chase. Brady followed her.

"Brady, go lie down in your bed." You'd have thought he'd taken away walks and his food dish by the look Brady gave him. But, doing the best Eeyore impression, the dog trudged over to his oversized, ergonomic dog bed. Nothing but the best for Brady.

Megan lifted her brow. "Brady? As in Tom Brady?" "God no. Blasphemy, woman. Not in my house."

She laughed. "Aw. I see. So, you must be a Cleveland or Cincinnati fan."

"Indianapolis Colts." He studied her for a moment. "But you didn't come all this way to discuss football or my dog. Quit stalling."

Megan sat on the sofa, and he took his favorite spot in an oversized recliner.

The silence between them was palpable. Finally, she reached into her bag and pulled out an envelope. She opened it and held up the contents.

He sighed. "How'd you find out?"

Her mouth dropped open as she shook her head. "Really? That's your first question? That's immaterial at this point. Since you didn't react with the same shock I did, I'm going to assume you knew about it. You have some explaining to do."

"Where did you get that?"

Ignoring his question, she said, "I admit, I hoped that you didn't remember the night any more than I did. So, why? Begin with telling me if it is real or a prank."

At that moment, he wanted to wrap her in his arms and protect her like he should have done two years ago. He wasn't sure how she'd react, though, so he stayed in his seat. A safe distance for both, because he could see the hurt and anger just fine from where he sat.

She crossed her arms over her chest. "I'm waiting."

He sighed, then took a deep, steadying breath. "Do you remember that morning in the hotel room?"

"Remembering that morning has never been a problem. It was the night before that's the issue."

"Okay, you got the call from someone almost immediately after we woke up. You found out that you won the Songbird contest or whatever. I don't remember the details—all I know is you were bursting with happiness. How could I ruin that?"

She glared. "Because. We. Got. Married." Megan said through gritted teeth.

He swallowed and nodded. How could he explain so she would understand?

"I thought embarrassment was the issue, and you didn't want to talk about it. I didn't know you had no memory of it, not at first, and figured we'd get around to a discussion. Then everything happened so fast.

"About the time you got that call, I realized you had no memory of the wedding. You said the opportunity meant everything to you. How there was no way you would go back to Lucky. You were adamant about that."

"So you're blaming me?"

He shook his head. "Of course not. I take full responsibility for the whole thing. I thought I was doing you a favor by not complicating your life with emotional baggage."

She frowned. "Our marriage is emotional baggage?"

"No." Shit, he couldn't win. He was making a bigger mess of things. No matter how he tried to explain it—it sounded bad.

Megan was silent for a long time. Then she finally opened her mouth, and Chase held his breath.

If he were honest, he'd like to get to know Megan better, without alcohol blurring the picture. And not because they were married, but because she was an intelligent, beautiful woman. She'd blown away by her five years before Vegas when she was home from school, and he ran into her at Joe's.

It had been after Connor's death. She put her sassiness on hold long enough to give him her heartfelt condolences. Though she was too young for him back then, she definitely made an impression.

Now he wanted Megan.

Take a chance.

Blowing out his breath, he said, "I'm sorry for all this. I'm sorry if my silence caused you embarrassment or grief. I'll do whatever you need or want me to do to make things easier for you."

She cocked her head. "But?"

"There's no but." He shook his head. "Not at all. I'd like to make it up to you. I'll buy you dinner and we can talk."

Her eyes widened. "Dinner? Dinner won't fix this. My God, we've been married for two years. What if I had gotten involved with someone? What if you met someone? How were you planning on handling that?"

He put his hands up. "I know, I know. But we stayed in touch with our texting and occasional calls. I figured you were too busy to get involved. I planned to tell you, but time got away from me. Then you were on the road touring and...." He let his voice drift off.

Finally, he said, "Please, let me take you to dinner. When are you flying back?"

Nibbling on her bottom lip, she said, "I was going to catch the last flight out today. I guess I could go back tomorrow. I took a few days off because of other things."

Her eyes dimmed. Would he be able to get her to talk about the asshole she'd been dealing with? He'd try for Kell's sake. And while he did that, he'd enjoy spending time with her.

"All right, but I'm keeping a low profile, remember? Having dinner in a restaurant isn't a smart idea if I want to leave town unnoticed."

"Let me worry about the venue. I promise to keep you under the radar of the good folks of Lucky."

She studied him for a moment. "Fine, you win. On one condition." She hesitated, holding up one, then two fingers. "No, two conditions."

Grinning, he laughed. "More conditions? A little haughty for a girl who used to beg for attention from her brother and me."

She stuck her tongue out. "Do you want to hear the conditions or not?"

He nodded. "Go on."

"Number one, we have to figure out how we're going to fix our problem, and number two, no alcoholic beverages. At least for me. Oh wait, three." She held up a third finger. "This is only a casual dinner between two old friends."

He raised a brow. "Jumping ahead of things, aren't you?"

"No, I don't think so, given our history."

"Point taken." He nodded. "All right, you've got yourself a deal."

Why had she agreed to dinner? She'd made a point of saying it was a casual *friend* dinner. But why? She'd. been dreaming about a date with Chase for as long as she could remember.

No. No, this was a friendly dinner. It couldn't be more than that. She needed to wrap things up in Lucky and get back to Nashville. Hopefully, Chase kept his promise about keeping it under the radar.

She could imagine Rich going ballistic if word got out. Having a clandestine dinner with a man would already be problematic. But if people found out the true reason for her visit to Lucky or about the marriage and the drunken night in Las Vegas....

Yes, her very opinionated manager would have plenty to say.

Truth be told, she was looking forward to spending time with Chase. That he wanted to spend time with her made her want to sing out with joy.

How long had she waited for him to notice her? Forever, it seemed.

She freshened up in his guest bathroom, and he was waiting for her when she walked back into the great room.

"So, where are we going? I doubt there is a place in Lucky where people won't recognize me."

He raised his brows. "Cocky, aren't you?"

"Not at all. Though I guess it sounded that way." She laughed. "Sorry, I didn't mean to sound arrogant. It was more about Mom being a lifelong, card-carrying member of Lucky's grapevine. I've never been able to go anywhere in this town without everyone knowing about it." She lowered her voice to a conspiratorial whisper, "Shh, she has spies everywhere." She grinned.

"It's a surprise. You'll see."

"Should I be nervous? Do I need a better disguise than a baseball cap and sunglasses?"

He smiled. "Not at all. You're perfect, just as you are."

The scene in *Bridget Jones's Diary* when Mark Darcy said "I like you very much, just as you are" flashed through Megan's mind. Acceptance was a rare commodity for celebrities. Sweeter, thinner, softer, kinder—whatever the day's critical assessment, it wore on a person.

Chase's comment warmed her heart.

The doorbell rang. "Stay here. I'll be right back." Brady started for the door, but Chase ordered, "Sit."

The dog whimpered but obeyed.

Chase came back into the room carrying a large basket.

"Now you've got my curiosity working overtime."

"It's the most private place I can think of, where there will be a zero chance of anyone seeing you. My boat."

"Smart. Who'd have thought you could be so sneaky?" She teased.

The color in his cheeks deepened. For years, she'd followed him around like a puppy waiting for a pat on her head, an act of kindness. Hell, she'd have been happy for any sign that he noticed her at all. Wait, that wasn't exactly true. He must have noticed her because he'd teased her all the time.

She enjoyed teasing him for a change.

"I thought we could take a slow ride around the lake this afternoon. Have a picnic supper later." He lifted his shoulders. "What do you think?"

Grinning, she said, "It's a fabulous idea. Thank you, Chase."

Megan yawned, stretching her arms above her head. She was lying on one of the padded bench seats on the pontoon. He sat on the opposite bench, facing her, legs extended, leaning against the backrest. She looked comfortable. Like she belonged. Perfect.

"I can't remember the last time I felt this relaxed. Look at all those stars." She sighed. "A girl could get used to this."

He wished that were true.

"Not that I expect—"

"I know what you meant."

The boat had carried them out far enough that they barely could hear the crickets or frogs. The water lapped against the side of the boat as the lightning bugs blinked in the still evening air. A soothing calm, Chase never grew tired of.

"I'm glad you're enjoying yourself. At the risk of *rocking the boat*"—he grinned—"we need to talk about how we're going to deal with our situation."

Normally, he would miss her eye roll and grin, but the full moon provided enough light.

"Oh, do we have to? Can't we float around all night as if we don't have a care in the world?"

"We could, but the problems will still be here—and eventually we'll run out of gas." He chuckled.

"Party pooper." She blinked and wedged herself up on her elbows. "Our marriage problem will still be here after we dock."

He hadn't decided how he was going to broach the subject of the asshole harassing her. He sure as hell didn't want to throw Kell under the bus for calling him about it. But weighing his options, it was better to be upfront. His last lie of omission didn't work out so well.

He moved to her side of the boat and nudged his way onto the bench beside her. The warmth of her body heated him where they touched.

"Kell called me."

Her eyes flew open and she scooted up so she was sitting rather than the lazy recline she'd been enjoying. "When? Is he all right?" Megan's voice escalated on each word.

When someone was overseas in harm's way, you didn't blurt something like that out. "Calm down. He's safe. It wasn't about him."

She clenched her fists and clamped her jaw.

"Listen." Chase held his hands out to stave off her anger. "Don't get all riled up. He called me yesterday. He's concerned about you. The phone call you two had didn't sit well with him. He's worried about that guy who doesn't understand the word no. Are you still having problems?"

The darkness of night didn't prevent Chase from seeing Megan's face pale. He took her hands into a firm clasp.

"What's going on? Talk to me."

"Why? It's not like you can do anything. You live hundreds of miles away. Besides, I've talked to the police—"

"The police. My God, what's going on?" He shook her hands. "Megan, tell me. Kell asked me to investigate. I was going to catch a flight first thing after I got off shift today and then you showed up here. How's that for irony?"

From her expression, she didn't appreciate his attempt at humor.

"Kell needs to realize I'm a grown woman. Your promise to him is no longer necessary."

"Bullshit."

She pulled her hands free and pushed him away until their bodies were no longer touching. He had to make her see that this was long past him feeling obligated.

"I want you to listen to me." She ducked her head to avoid looking at him, but he cupped her chin, so they were eye to eye.

"Look at me. Yes, I promised your brother I'd watch out for you when he left. Hell, you were a kid. But you're right—you're a grown woman. Now I want to look out for you because I want to do it. Not for Kell. Not for Ruby. For you.

"You mean something to me. After Las Vegas, I tried to put what happened between us out of my mind. I should have known that was never gonna happen. I knew I'd have to face you with the truth someday. And I haven't been able to get you out of my head. Not even a little. Do you understand?

"Every time your song comes on the radio, I'm sucked right back to our night together. I'm not sure how much longer I would have been able to go on without contacting you in person. Fuck the texts.

"You're important to me. And if I can help protect you, I will." He inhaled, then blew it out.

Megan sat wide-eyed; her mouth shaped in a perfect O. A slow grin grew on her face. "That's the most I've ever heard you say at one time."

It took Chase a moment to realize she was teasing. He smiled, tucking a strand of her hair behind her ear. "And this is the longest you've been quiet."

Lightning-fast, he pulled her to him. Placing his hand under the mass of auburn curls, he cradled her neck and drew her face to within mere inches of his. He caressed her cheek with his thumb and forefinger. Circling her mouth, he focused his attention on her lips.

He moved in, so his mouth almost touched hers. Leisurely, he claimed her lips, then dipped her head back giving him better access to her jawline. He kissed his way along until a whispered gasp rewarded him when he found a sweet spot under her earlobe. He explored her neckline until the need for her lips drew him back to her mouth.

With his mouth on hers again, he stroked his tongue along her lips. Teasing at the seam. Finally, he swept his tongue into her mouth, ramping up the kiss.

She reciprocated the motion, and he moaned. Intertwined, their tongues swirled. until he withdrew so he could go back to nibbling along her jaw.

When he pulled away, he was breathing hard. She straightened and blew out a breath as she combed her hands through her hair.

Chase stood and adjusted himself. Then he leaned down to her face and whispered, "I want you, Megan. I'm all in. Kissing is great. But I want more. When we have sex again, it will be under ideal circumstances.

Romantic music, dimmed lights, a little wine, and you and me naked in my king bed. We'll do it right this time and we won't forget a single detail."

She stared at him.

"And I did say when, not if. Because it's gonna happen."

Chapter 9

Chase steered the boat back to his dock in silence.

Would she confide in him and allow him to help her? They still hadn't discussed Vegas. Neither of them had mentioned an annulment or divorce. In either case, he was hopeful they could work through it and come out

together on the other side.

Megan didn't say anything until her phone buzzed back at his house. "Sorry."

He checked his watch. "It's late for a call."

She shrugged. "It's my manager, Rich. I need to take it."

"Take your time. Come here, Brady. Leave the lady alone, boy." Poor Brady didn't understand why he didn't get to go out on the boat like he usually did. So now he was desperate for attention. "I'll be in the kitchen if you need me."

She wandered into the kitchen ten minutes later, nibbling her bottom lip. A nervous habit he usually found both endearing and erotic. But tonight, he could see something was wrong.

"What's going on? Come sit."

Sitting on one of the four stools at his breakfast bar, she held up two fingers. "Two things. First, he doesn't want us to do anything about the marriage."

She air quoted the word *marriage*. "Not yet anyway. Rich doesn't want the negative publicity. I guess it's bad enough that Nashville's latest sweetheart had a drunken night in Vegas and ended up hitched. But a divorce might make it worse." She shook her head. "It's lame. If they can't like and appreciate me for my music, then screw them."

Her voice shook as she spoke, and she was still attacking her lower lip. Was that false bravado he heard in her voice?

"You said two things."

"Oh, right. Buttercup got vandalized last night."

Blinking, he asked, "Who or what's a Buttercup?"

He came around the counter and sat on the stool next to her.

"My yellow Volkswagen bug. I named her Buttercup."

"Okay. What happened to your car?"

"I left the car in the lot at the studio. I went home with my assistant, Brenda. She's watching my cat while I'm here. I had such an early flight, it made sense for me to stay at her place. She took me to the airport early this morning."

He nodded. "How much damage?"

Megan bowed her head. "Bad. He painted the word bitch on the driver's door, among other ugly words and drawings."

"He? How do they know it's a man?"

She looked up, shaking her head. The nervous bounce of her leg began, and he put his hand on her thigh to still her leg.

"It's all right. Tell me."

She ducked her head, mumbling, "Oh, this is the real swell part. He jacked off on the car."

"Shit."

"No, thank God he didn't do that, too."

They looked at each other, and a nervous giggle escaped her lips. He grinned. Chase loved her sense of humor. Pulling her onto his lap, he wrapped her in a tight hug.

"At least I've still got my sense of humor, right?"

"Yes, you do, and I've always loved that about you."

"You have?"

"I have."

"Chase, don't take these next two requests the wrong way." This time she didn't indicate the numbers with her fingers.

"First conditions and now requests. Wow, you're a demanding woman."

Shrugging, she said, "Part of my charm. Anyway, first, if you have any wine in the house, I could use a glass to calm my nerves."

So much for the no alcohol declaration. Perfectly understandable.

He shifted her back to her stool. "Your wish is my command. Red or white?"

"White would be great. If you have it."

He moved around the counter. Reaching into his wine fridge, he pulled out a bottle of pinot grigio. Is this all right?

"That will be wonderful. Thanks."

As he was pouring the wine, she asked her second request.

"Can I sleep here tonight?"

Wine splashed over the rim of the glass and onto the counter.

She put her hand up, amending, "Of course, strictly platonic. I can stay in a guest room. I assume you must have a guest room in this big house."

He mopped up the spill and handed her the glass. "Yeah, there's a guest room. Two, in fact. Although I use one as my home office."

She continued with her explanation as if she hadn't heard him.

"I don't want to explain to my mom why I'm here for such a quick trip. She'll ask a million questions and won't let up until she knows everything.

I'd like to keep the whole drunken night at the Chapel of Bliss away from the Lucky grapevine, if possible. At least for now. I guess it will eventually come out."

He exhaled a breath he hadn't realized he was holding. At least he could put off a confrontation with Ruby for a while longer. There'd be hell to pay when she learned the truth, since she sent him to Vegas to keep Megan safe from men.

And wait until Megan found out that Ruby sent him.

Don't think about that right now.

"Unless it's a bother or you're afraid you won't be able to resist my charm?" She fluttered her long lashes at him.

Challenge accepted.

"I can control myself," he said. "For now." She studied him over the top of her wineglass.

Finally, she nodded. "Okay, thanks for letting me stay and the warning."

Was that a smirk she hid behind her glass of wine?

The doorbell rang as Megan was finally falling asleep. What time was it? She didn't want to turn on the light to look at her watch. Brady's barking began almost immediately.

The poor dog had pouted when Chase shooed him from her room earlier. She wouldn't have minded the company, but rules were rules, and Brady was not allowed on the beds.

The doorbell rang three more times before she saw a line of light appear under the door. She heard Chase stumble down the hall, with Brady leading the charge.

Crap, who dropped by at this hour?

Whoever it was sure wasn't patient. The ringing finally stopped. Curiosity might have killed the cat, but the hushed voices were too tempting for Megan to ignore.

Grinning, she channeled her younger self. Spying on Chase and Kell had been her favorite extracurricular activity. She climbed out of bed and tiptoed down the hall and down the stairs. She didn't dare stick her head around the corner. Whoever it was would spot her.

She could hear it was a woman because she wasn't speaking in hushed tones at all, despite Chase shushing her.

"Sherry, you've been drinking. Did you drive out here alone?"

"How else would I get here? You forgot our date tonight." Wow, the pouty whine in the woman's voice echoed all the way to where Megan was eavesdropping at the bottom of the stairs.

Wait. A date? Was he involved with someone? She ran a replay of everything they'd said and done since she got there. Never did he say anything about another woman.

And the way he kissed me ...

Hell, they'd been making out like teenagers and would have done more than kiss if he hadn't stopped them. Is that why he stopped? She hated the suspicion and doubt that skipped around in her head.

"We didn't have a date, Sherry. You're a sweet kid, but like I've told you more than once, I'm not interested in dating."

Megan blew out the breath she didn't realize she was holding. Glad to hear him say that.

"Hey, whose car is that in your driveway? Is it a rental?"

"Shit," he muttered.

"Shit," Megan whispered.

"A friend is visiting from out of town. It's late. We need to keep our voices down."

"A female friend?"

"That's none of your business."

"Is she why you won't go out with me again?" The woman's whining was annoying.

"Again?" he said in a louder tone. "Sherry, it wasn't a date. I drove you home from Joe's one time, because you were tipsy. Nothing happened. It looks like I'm going to have to take your keys and drive you home again."

"Nah, don't worry about it."

"Give me your keys." Megan heard shuffling and grunting.

"You're no fun."

"I'll be right back. I'm going to throw on a T-shirt and grab my keys. Don't move."

"Don't get dressed on my account." She giggled.

Megan sprinted up the stairs, down the hall, and into the bedroom so Chase wouldn't catch her being nosy. She closed the door and leaned her back against it, breathing hard.

Shit, girl you need to get back to the gym and those cardio workouts.

Megan searched her memory bank but couldn't remember a Sherry from school. The woman was definitely younger than Megan and much younger than Chase. Hadn't he called her a sweet kid?

Seems like younger women had a weakness for him. She sure did.

Lost in her thoughts, she shrieked at the sharp rap on the door. Her hands flew to her chest, and she willed her heart to calm down as Chase pushed open the door with ease, sliding her with it.

"Psst, in case you missed anything from the conversation, I'm running Sherry home. She's been drinking, and I can't let her drive. Go back to bed. I'll be back in fifteen."

Ignoring him, she said, "Oh my God, Chase. You scared me to death. How am I supposed to sleep now? My heart is racing like crazy."

She walked to the bathroom and flipped on the light so she could see him better.

"You'll be fine." He grinned. "Though you might want to work on your spying skills. You've gotten rusty over the years." Chuckling, he headed to his room.

Interesting. This Sherry gal was smitten. Megan couldn't blame her. She knew all too well what it was like to have a crush on Chase. To admire him from afar, hoping for a crumb of attention.

She punched her pillow and tugged the sheet, trying to get comfortable, and closed her eyes. But she couldn't shut off her thoughts.

She popped up, eyes wide, staring into the darkness of the room. "I'm married to him."

The realization and all it meant finally hit her. How many times had she doodled Mrs. Chase Devine, Megan Devine, and Mr. and Mrs. Devine in her teenage journals? Too many to count, for sure.

Hmm.

Chapter 10

Shit, his house felt empty.

How was it possible that Megan's presence had taken such a hold in less than twenty-four hours? Even his recliner that he usually lived in was too lumpy and uncomfortable. He roamed from room to room, cursing ever bringing her into his home.

Brady sulked. Lifting his head, his eyes questioned, "Why did you make her leave? I liked her."

So did Chase, damn it.

This house was his inner sanctum. His retreat when his job heated up, literally. He'd designed and built it to meet all his specifications. Now it felt like a box he was trapped in.

So, what are you going to do about it?

He wanted Megan back here. With him. But that was impossible. Her career was in Nashville, and his was here in Lucky.

He'd always been able to keep a safe emotional distance except when he heard her on the radio. But overall, he'd been doing fine.

But now he couldn't stop thinking about her. Was this what addiction felt like? He understood that, like most addictions, what he was feeling wasn't healthy. He'd focus on something else. If he did that, a solution would come to him. Careful consideration was necessary because their actions affected other people. Was it fair to either of them with so many complications?

Yeah, that ship has sailed.

Whether he wanted to admit it or not, Vegas had changed both their lives. For now, he would respect her wishes. He wouldn't pursue an annulment or divorce until she gave the go-ahead. For them to have any kind of chance at a real and lasting relationship, they needed to start over. Wash the slate clean.

And then he needed a plan.

Though it did feel a little like closing the barn door after the cows had already gotten out, as his Gramps used to say. How could they rewind back to the dating stage?

Nashville

Megan hadn't heard from Chase in the week since she'd been back. Not that she expected she would. A small part of her—oh come on, a big part of her—hoped he would call.

The phone lines work both ways.

Rich and the publicist were still pushing for the low-profile angle. So far, she was following their lead, but at some point, she and Chase would have to make some kind of decision, do something.

It concerned Rich that the copy of the marriage license ended up with him unexpectedly. They needed to investigate that aspect. Whoever sent it could send it to the news media, in which case the publicist's work wouldn't be able to fix it.

"Good night," Megan called, waving to her friends. It had been a productive but exhausting day at the recording studio. She'd stopped for a beer and a bite at one of their favorite downtown honkytonks on Broadway Street.

All she wanted was home and a hot shower—her bed was calling her name. She craved her evening cuddle time with Emmie, too.

Colorful neon lights danced on the sidewalk. She took care to step over the "break your momma's back" cracks as she hustled to her car.

Turning the corner, she frowned, realizing how far she'd parked. In daylight, it hadn't seemed that far—in darkness, it was a hike. Because of the happy hour crowds, she'd had to park three blocks away, and down an alley.

Gone were the neon lights on Broadway. The song lyrics popped in her head, as lyrics often did, and any other time they would have brought a smile to her face.

Not tonight.

Shivering despite the warm night, she couldn't shake the feeling that someone was watching her. She picked up her pace. The awareness intensified the closer she got to her car. That full belly now felt like lead in the pit of her stomach. She glanced over her shoulder, her Spidey-sense in overdrive.

How had she managed to park under the only streetlight not working tonight? Odd. Should she turn around and go back to the restaurant?

Don't be silly. The car is right here.

Unlocking the car with the key fob, she reached for the handle—sighing in relief.

Wham.

Her body slammed against the car with such force it took her breath from her lungs. Instinctively, she gulped for air, and panic swept over her when she couldn't catch her breath. Dizziness threatened to overtake her.

The momentum caused her head to smash into the window. *Whack.* Her whole face throbbed, and the metallic taste of blood flooded her tongue. The contact had cut her upper lip.

A man's arm wrapped around her shoulders and crushed her neck. He was able to cover her mouth with his hand, which made screaming impossible even if she could catch her breath. Pain vibrated down her neck and spine.

A familiar, cloying scent toyed with her memory. A cologne?

He pressed his body into her, keeping her pinned against the car. She tried to twist and turn, but the more she struggled, the tighter he squeezed, crushing her trachea. Her eyes watered from the pain.

"We're gonna take a little stroll around the corner of the building to my car. Nice and slow. Do you understand?"

That voice. She recognized it immediately. Jason Sykes.

She didn't answer, and he squeezed his arm tighter around her throat. She managed a tiny nod, and he loosened his grip enough for her to take a raspy breath.

Relax. Stay calm.

If he took her someplace, her chance of survival wasn't good.

"Okay, bitch, here we go. Don't try anything. I won't hesitate to squeeze this pretty little neck of yours until you can't sing another note."

She tried to remember the self-defense lessons Kell and Chase taught her. She needed to be ready.

Sykes took a step back.

Forcing her body to relax, she went completely limp, pretending to lose consciousness.

Taking advantage of his hesitation, in a single deft move, she twisted her body and slammed her knee up into his balls. He dropped his hands to protect the family jewels, and she stomped on his foot. After grinding the heel of her boot until he cried out, she aimed another kick to his knee.

Then she ran. Retraced her steps back toward the restaurant. She opened her mouth to scream, but no sound came out.

She looked over her shoulder.

He wasn't following her. "You can run, bitch," he yelled, the sound echoing off the pavement and darkened buildings, "but I'll find you. I'll always find you." The freak nut-job pounded his fist on the hood of the car.

Rounding the corner, she ran faster, stealing one more look over her shoulder to make sure he wasn't on her tail. Whipping around, she crashed right into a group of people exiting the bar. People surrounded her. There was lots of commotion and a chorus of comments.

"Is she okay?"

"What happened to her?"

"Look at her face. She's bleeding."

Someone finally shouted, "Call 911. I think she's been attacked."

Don't leave me.

Her adrenaline sapped, she collapsed to the sidewalk as blackness swept over her.

Chapter 11

Nashville

"Damn that bitch," Jason swore as he limped into his apartment. Megan had hit her mark. He was still nauseous, and although he hadn't vomited, he was sore as hell. The pain was worse in his foot and knee.

The throbbing in his foot hadn't let up at all. But he was most concerned that she might have broken his kneecap with that last kick. He sure as hell couldn't go to a hospital to get checked out.

Suck it up.

He'd stop at a drugstore to pick up what he needed after he got on the road. For now, he grabbed his computer and to-go bag he kept packed for quick escapes, ripped his favorite pictures from his wall, and was out of his apartment in less than fifteen minutes. The police would come, but he figured he had a little bit of time.

He rubbed his knee as he drove. The pain reminded him of the time when he was six and broke his arm falling off the monkey bars. His mom wouldn't take him to the hospital. He'd had to suffer through the pain for weeks.

It wasn't broken, you baby. It was just a sprain.

He ignored the voice in his head.

Why had Megan resisted him? He would have given her everything. He loved her more than anyone ever could. Especially more than the loser she married.

What a joke. That wasn't a marriage.

She's a tramp. Mama wouldn't approve.

"Shut up," he screamed as he flipped on the radio and turned up the volume.

After she wouldn't give him the time of day after all the gifts, he'd tried to frighten her—the rat had been brilliant. But she didn't turn to him for comfort. No, instead she sealed her fate when she went to the cops and got him fired.

He hadn't followed her to abduct her. He'd only wanted a chance to talk to her. He had planned to bring her to his apartment so she could see how much she meant to him.

He'd regroup and think of a new plan. A better plan. It was only a matter of time before Megan would be his.

Chapter 12

Lucky

Chase was finishing up in the kitchen with two probies. The rest of the crew sat in front of a fifty-inch TV, catching up on the news, waiting for their daily dose of *Jeopardy* to come on. Nothing like a little friendly competition between fellow firefighters. God help anyone who suggested they turn the channel.

"Hey, Cap, get over here. You need to see this," shouted Sparky. Ron Sparks had joined the fire department around the same time as Chase.

Chase dropped the dish towel on the counter and jogged over to the men. "What's up?" He stopped short and his eyes widened as a headshot of Megan appeared on the screen.

"Nashville singer attacked... hospitalized..." Chase strained to hear. "Turn it up."

"Megan Howard was allegedly attacked around eleven last night in downtown Nashville. The police haven't released any details yet..."

Chase already had his phone in hand, dialing Ruby's number.

A half hour later, he knew little more. Megan's assistant had called Ruby to let her know about the attack. Apparently, Megan had been out having drinks with friends at a honkytonk in the Music Row area of Nashville. Ruby had been trying to reach the hospital with no success.

Because of her extreme fear of flying, Ruby asked Chase to fly down, and he was on the first flight the next day. He'd be in Nashville before noon.

Even if Ruby hadn't asked him to go, Chase had already been packing his bag.

He went directly to the hospital, bypassing the initial red tape by identifying himself as Megan's husband, providing his copy of their marriage certificate for proof.

It wasn't a lie. A well-known truth, it was not.

But if there was ever a time he was grateful, they were still legally married, this would be it.

He stopped in the doorway of her darkened hospital room. Her small, prone body brought him up short. Asleep, she looked so young. So vulnerable.

"Fuck," he swore under his breath. He swallowed several times as his heart raced, and he clenched his fists by his sides.

A doctor filled him in on her list of injuries. The list included a laceration to her right temple and a contusion to her right cheek. There were several other less severe cuts and bruises. But the doctor's primary concern was her larynx.

Until the internal inflammation subsided, and they could determine the level of damage to her larynx, the doctor did not want Megan to use her voice. Which might explain why there was a notepad and pen on the adjacent table.

Damn. The bastard had strangled her.

What would she do if she couldn't sing again? He shook the thought away. Megan needed him to be positive and strong, so that's what he planned to be.

He stepped closer to her bedside. A bandage covered the lacer-ation on her forehead. Even in the dim light, the bruising on her cheek and the marks on her neck screamed at him, pronounced and ugly. He still had clenched hands, and he sure as hell was ready to hit something or someone.

He left her to sleep and walked down to the waiting room for a cup of coffee. As he sipped, he took in his surroundings. There was a petite woman speaking to a couple of cops next to the nurse's station.

After the cops left, he approached the woman.

"Excuse me. I couldn't help but overhear. Are you Brenda Hines, by any chance?"

Her eyes narrowed. "Yes," she said, her voice so tentative, he wasn't sure she knew herself. But he was a stranger. Of course, she'd be reluctant after what happened to Megan.

"Sorry, I didn't mean to frighten you. I'm a friend from back home. From Lucky." He held his hand out. "I'm Chase Devine."

As if a lightbulb clicked on, she said, "You're Chase? I'm so glad you're here." She shook his hand.

"You know who I am?"

"Yes. Not at first, but after the marriage license appeared, Megan confided in me." Grinning, she put her hand up to her mouth and stage-whispered, "You're the husband."

"Yep. I am." He shrugged. "I don't think whispering is neces-sary since I identified myself as Megan's husband to the hospital staff."

"You did? Oh, my. Rich's going to have a fit."

"He's her manager, right?"

She nodded. "Yep. But regardless of how he feels, I'm glad you came. She's going to need all the support and care we can give her. If I ever see that asshole again, I will... I will... well, it isn't ladylike to say what I'd like to cut off with my granddad's hunting knife."

"You'll have to stand in line."

Brenda gave him a little smile. She filled in the gaps of the sketchy details he'd gotten from Ruby. Megan had identified her attacker as the man who had been stalking her. The cops put out an APB and raided his apartment, but the guy was in the wind.

Chase didn't trust the police or hospital staff to keep her safe. It seemed like the police were already on defense rather than offense.

Megan was a sitting duck here. Hell, she couldn't even scream for help. When she got released, he would — His phone vibrated with an unknown number on the display screen. It could be Megan's doctor.

"Devine," he answered.

"What the hell happened?"

"Kell, hey, you talked to your mom?"

"Yeah, but you know my mom. Long on drama and short on details. What do you know?"

Chase gave Kell the facts about the attack, his sister's injuries, and what the police were doing. "Shit, I should be there."

"I've got it covered. I jumped on a plane early this morning and have been here at the hospital for a couple of hours now."

"Thanks. Have you talked to her?"

"Not yet. She's been asleep. She looks pretty beat-up."

"Fuck."

"Exactly what I said when I walked into her room. I intend to stick around and take care of her."

"I know, but I wish I could be there for her."

"Listen, I don't know when they'll release her. But when they do, I want to bring her back to Lucky with me."

"You think she should leave Nashville?"

"As long as the cops and doctors give the go-ahead, yes, I do. The asshole who attacked her is still out there. She'll be safer back home."

"Then yeah, I agree."

"I'm not sure she won't pull her bull-headed stubbornness and refuse to go."

"You've got that right. She can be a stubborn brat." There was a smile in Kell's voice.

They were silent for a second. Then Kell continued, "I appreciate you looking out for her. I guess she's like a little sister to you, too."

What could he say to that? Nothing could be further from the truth. He didn't think of Megan as a little sister. At all.

If he was honest with himself, he'd admit that his feelings for Megan had changed even before Las Vegas.

How could he tell his friend what had happened? It seemed like the window of opportunity slammed shut on that a long time ago.

"Chase?"

Chase shook his head. "Yeah, I'm here. Sorry. Got distracted for a minute. Lots of activity here in the hospital."

"I get it. I asked if she can talk."

"The doctors don't want her to use her voice at all until the swelling goes down. Even then, she'll need to see a specialist about her larynx."

"Damn, I wanted to call her."

"I'm happy to relay back and forth, but I think that would frustrate her."

"You're probably right. Tell her I called. Okay? It's killing me that I'm not able to be there for her in person."

"Of course. You keep your head down and eyes open."

"Oorah."

The line went dead, and Chase stuffed his phone into his jacket pocket. Pushing off from the wall, he walked to Megan's room. Hopefully, he'd be able to convince her that his idea was the right thing to do. The sooner he could take her to Lucky where he could protect her, the sooner he could relax.

Chapter 13

Megan trudged through her nightmare. As much as she tried to get away, she couldn't. No matter how fast she tried to move, she felt as if she was mired in mud.

Plagued with pain and fear, she awoke, damp with perspiration. Someone had hurt her. But now a sense of calm seeped into her body. The nightmare morphed into a floating, dreamlike state where she felt safe.

Someone was whispering to her. She couldn't quite make out the words, but there was a deep, encouraging cadence. She recognized the voice. Didn't she?

Lying still, with her eyes closed, she allowed her other senses to absorb her surroundings. A gentle pressure on her hand. A butterfly wisp of something brushing across her cheek. She concentrated on the whispers. But they seemed so far away.

"I'm here now. I'll take care of you. I won't let anyone hurt you again."

It sounded so much like Chase. Oh, how she wished it could be Chase. It had to be a dream, though. He was hundreds of miles away, back home in Lucky.

"Megan, can you hear me?" The murmurs were getting louder.

Megan? Someone knew her name.

Her eyes fluttered open, and there was Chase, leaning down with a warm smile. He held one of her hands and brushed a stray strand of hair from her cheek with his other.

She opened her mouth to speak, but he rushed to say, "Don't." He put his finger to his lips. "Your larynx was injured. The doctors do not want you to use your voice until the swelling subsides."

Then he squeezed her hand even tighter. "Don't be afraid. I'm not leaving you. There's a notepad and a pen when you want to communicate. Understand?"

She managed a slight nod. Sleep was overtaking her again; she couldn't keep her eyes open. But she wasn't afraid—she could feel Chase's hand squeezing hers. Now that she was safe, she relaxed and drifted to sleep.

Several hours later, Chase stepped out while the doctor checked on her and explained her injuries. Bruised and achy, she gingerly touched her throat. They hoped it wouldn't be permanent. But the doctor wasn't willing to say with any certainty that she would recover 100 percent.

Time would tell.

Fear was the worst part. She was scared that she couldn't perform anymore. That she would lose the career she'd worked so hard to build. There was also the constant fear that Jason could get to her again.

Megan stared out at the rain pouring down, a gloomy day to match her mood. The only thing that gave her peace was having Chase nearby. She wasn't sure how long he'd be able to stay. He couldn't put his life on permanent hold to be there for her.

Chase didn't want Megan returning to her apartment alone after her discharge the next day.

After the cops filled him in on the extent of Sykes's crazy obsession, Chase was even more concerned for her safety. He could stay for a few more days, but he had to get back to Lucky. And it would be easier to protect her away from Nashville.

Behind a locked door in his apartment, the sick guy had a shrine to Megan. Photos of her covered the walls. Clear proof he had been stalking her for months. Sykes had somehow even gotten into Megan's apartment and rigged a camera in her bedroom.

They collected DNA to compare with the semen from the incident with her car. Chase didn't need to wait for the results. He wanted Megan as far away from that sicko as he could get her. But he dreaded the argument ahead.

She was sitting up in bed when he entered her room.

"What did the doctor say? Did he sign the discharge papers?" Chase asked.

She didn't respond immediately—in fact, when he looked closer, she had tears in her eyes.

"Hey, hey, what's wrong?" He sat on the edge of her bed, wiping away the streaks of her tears with his thumb.

She took the small notepad and pen from her lap and wrote: *Nothing. Just feeling sorry for myself. Ignore me. Yes, the doctor signed the discharge papers.*

"Then I'm busting you out of this joint."

She put her head down, hiding her eyes from him as she wrote: *I'm afraid.*

Shit. She was breaking his heart. He tried to pull her into his arms without hurting her.

"Megan, I need to talk to you. Kell and I talked and—"

She stiffened and pushed away from his embrace. Shaking her head, she grabbed the notepad and scribbled: *Don't talk about me with Kell. Don't want to worry him.*

"I'm sorry, babe, your mom already told him. Come on, you know Kell will worry, especially over you. But he's smart. He'll take care of himself."

She continued shaking her head. Her left hand fisted in the sheet.

He plowed on. "But if you want to ease some of his worry, I have an idea."

Her eyes narrowed. She motioned with her hand for him to continue.

"I want you to come back to Lucky with me. You'll be able to recuperate without worrying about Sykes lurking around every corner. You currently can't sing, so your job is on a temporary hiatus. It's the perfect place to build your strength and heal."

He almost saw her wheels turning. He held his breath. Finally, she looked him in the eye and nodded.

His brows lifted. "Yes? Just like that, you agreed?"

She wrote: *Don't act so surprised. I want to get far away until the police find him. No more plotting with Kell. Got it?*

He nodded as he saluted. "I got it."

"Are you sure you want to stay with your mom? Do you think you can get the proper rest there? I know you and your mom don't always get along." Brenda asked as she was helping Megan dress after being discharged.

I hope so. It's my home. Maybe it will be a chance for us to get closer.

Brenda raised her brow. "Okay, I'm sure we could figure out something else."

Her energy waning, Megan sat on the side of her bed and scribbled: *No, I think it will be fine.*

"If that's what you want. I'm sorry you can't take Emmie."

Megan frowned and wrote, "Mom's cat allergy is extreme. Otherwise, I would pack the little fur ball along with my clothes.

"Well, you know I will take good care of her."

I know. That's why I'm leaving her with you.

Chase walked into the room a few minutes later. "Okay, ladies, ready to go? I'll pull my rental up to the door."

Both women nodded. "I'll follow you in my car," Brenda said.

Chase clapped his hands. "Sounds like a plan."

Chapter 14

Nashville

Chase leaned against the counter that separated Megan's kitchen and living room. Rich Reynolds was throwing his managerial weight around and causing chaos, while Brenda gave Megan a hand packing up so they could leave first thing in the morning.

He liked the petite woman who had Megan's back. She had spunk and a big heart.

He'd lend a hand, too, but thought it best to stay out of the way for the time being. Too many cooks in the kitchen, as Grandma Devine used to say. Besides, he had no idea what she'd need or want during her convalescence. He'd leave that up to Brenda's expertise. When the time comes, he'll lend a hand, loading it all into her car. But when Megan stumbled, he jumped into action, catching her and lowering her to the sofa before she hit the floor.

She leaned back, closing her eyes and whispered, "Sorry. Lightheaded."

"Megan Howard." Brenda admonished. "No talking. Remember the doctor's orders." Megan gave her a thumbs-up but kept her eyes closed.

"I'm going to make you a cup of tea before we finish the packing. We've got all your must-haves packed. I'll do a quick check around the bedroom and bathroom, too."

Chase sat on the coffee table, his knees bracketing hers. "You realize we have stores in Ohio? We can get you anything you might forget. We aren't going to the moon."

"I know," she mouthed, with no sound.

"Okay, I'm going to head out, Megan," Reynolds announced. "This is for the best. Lemonade from lemons. It'll get you out of the spotlight until you're back on your feet. Oh, I'll let you know when we decide how to spin your Vegas marriage in a positive light. For now, keeping a low profile is best."

Chase wanted to pummel the guy for his insensitivity and was glad when he left.

There was a teary goodbye between Megan and her little gray cat. Chase and Megan were leaving early, so it only made sense to send Emmie home with Brenda now.

The tears continued as Brenda and Megan hugged and said their goodbyes. Their relationship went beyond that of a typical employer and employee.

Megan looked beat. She said good night and headed to her bedroom.

Chase settled onto the sofa, stretching to get comfortable, when he heard a sound coming from her bedroom. He tapped on the door and opened it slowly. "Megan, everything okay?"

Light filtered in through the curtains. She sat huddled in the middle of her bed. The bruising was still prominent on her pale skin.

She sniffled. Fear and exasperation played on her face. She began to write something on the notepad but stopped, sighed, then threw the pad and pen across the room.

She shook her head. In a whisper barely loud enough for him to hear, she said, "I can't stop shaking." Her voice cracked as she cried. "I'm sorry."

"Shh. Don't talk and don't be sorry." He took a step inside the room but didn't dare go farther. There was every reason a man could spook her right now. His heart ached for Megan. She didn't deserve to be in this situation.

He slowly moved farther into the room and picked up the pad and pen from the floor. He handed it to her then turned on the bedside lamp.

She wrote: *I'm so angry. He had a camera here.* She shuddered. *I feel violated. This is my home.*

Through her tears and sniffles, she wrote: *Could you stay with me, just until I fall asleep?*

Chase blew out his breath. "Of course I will." He moved to the edge of her bed. "I'll sit right here." Then he patted the bed beside him. "Lie down. I'll keep you safe. I promise." She did as he instructed.

Tentatively, so not to startle her, he touched her arm and soothed her. When he felt her relax under his touch, he moved his hand to her head and brushed her hair away from her face. Soon he heard the even breathing of sleep. He slowly slipped off the bed, tucked the sheet around her, and left the room, leaving the door cracked.

❧

The decision to drive instead of flying was simple.

She'd need a vehicle in Lucky. Besides, she'd packed enough stuff for a year. He'd drive straight through and hope she wouldn't get too tired. But since he had to be back at work tomorrow afternoon, they didn't have much choice.

Her little Volkswagen Bug, Buttercup, had a fresh coat of paint after the vandalism. Chase noticed right away that there was surprising head and leg room, ample enough for his six-foot-two frame. But like most compact cars, the two front seats were close. There was much more room in the cab of his F-150, but he sure didn't mind being near Megan for the next seven hours.

The coconut scent of her shampoo reminded him of the beach. The temptation to reach across the console to take her small, fragile hand in his was great. Instead, he gripped the steering wheel tighter. She was recovering from a violent crime and in no condition for another guy pawing at her.

"You know this is a first," Chase said when they were underway, heading north out of the city on I-65. Megan glanced his way, cocking her head. "This is the first time, in all the years I've known you, that you won't be able to talk back or start an argument." He winked at her and chuckled.

She grabbed the notepad and pen from the center console.

He took a quick glance over to see what she wrote.

Ha. You think you're so funny.

Laughing outright now, he said, "Yep. I guess I do."

Even without my voice, I'll still give you crap.

"I have no doubt at all." He grinned.

She folded her arms across her chest and sighed. Her eyelids closed. She'd probably fallen asleep. She was so exhausted.

She surprised him by reaching across the console, tapping his arm. He glanced over and she mouthed, "Thank you for last night."

He nodded and squeezed her hand. "Anytime."

After a few more miles, he said, "Why don't you put your seat back? Take a nap. We've got a long drive ahead of us."

She gave him a thumbs-up.

He smiled when she closed her eyes. She was asleep the next time he glanced over.

Megan woke when the motion stopped. She looked around and opened her mouth to speak before she remembered her situation. She cringed when she swallowed, and a sharp pain shot through her throat.

"Hey there. We're in Cincinnati," Chase said. "I stopped for gas and a bite to eat. You've got to be hungry, right?"

She nodded and gave him another thumbs-up. Wow, that painkiller she'd taken before they left Nashville had knocked her out.

She scooted her seat up and stretched her arms above her head and checked the mirror. She wore a light fashion scarf around her neck to cover the bandage. Megan fluffed her hair to hide the one on her forehead.

"You look beautiful." Chase winked at her.

Her stomach growled, drawing his attention as he opened her door. He grinned. "Yeah, I'm hungry, too." He reached in and placed his hand on her arm to help her out, causing her entire body to warm to his touch.

Once they were settled in a booth, she took the pad out of her bag. *Sorry I haven't been very good company.* She drew a sad face next to her words.

"Nah, don't worry about it. This is cool. I enjoy hanging with you. To tell you the truth, the quiet is nice. Tomorrow I'll be wishing I was back here with you. Generally, there's a lot of commotion at the fire station. This has been peaceful.

"Not that it's been peaceful for you," he rushed to add. "I just meant that being with you feels good."

Chase ordered for them both, after Megan jotted down that she wanted herbal tea with some fresh fruit. While they waited for the food to arrive, Megan wrote: *You love being a firefighter? Don't you?*

"Yeah, I do. It's what I've wanted to do for what seems like my entire life. After Conner died, I was even more determined to make it happen." After a thoughtful pause, he continued, "You know a lot of the history since you were around when I first started working at the fire station."

Before thinking she started to write *I used to ride my bike...*

She stopped and scribbled over what she had written. Her neck and face warmed. Why not blurt out that he's been your crush from the time you were old enough to know boys were different from girls?

Chase placed his hand over hers. "What were you going to write?"

She shrugged.

Scribbling: *I used to ride my bike past the station in the summer, hoping to see you.*

"I remember seeing you. I don't know how much you remember. You're so much younger. I used to hang out at your house all the time because my house wasn't a very fun place to be after Conner died."

She nodded.

"Saving lives so other families don't have to lose a loved one ... that's why I love what I do so much. If I can save another family from that kind of pain, that's why I do it."

She drew another sad face and jotted: *I'm sorry about Conner.*

She reached across the table and gave his hand a quick squeeze.

"Thanks."

He seemed to want to talk, so Megan listened. She wanted to hear about his family, his past, and his decisions. He was right; she'd been too young when he came home with Kell, but she remembered him being around. The funny thing was, she'd never thought of him as another brother. Never.

"My mom can't understand my way of thinking or my career choice. You'd think at nearly thirty-two I wouldn't get a lecture every time I go home," he said with a self-deprecating chuckle.

"She can't understand how I can get anywhere near a fire. The car Conner was in exploded in fire after he hit a tree. But it's because of how he died that I am even more committed."

He fidgeted with the utensils on the table, lining up the knife, fork, and spoon vertically in front of him.

"And of course, there's the whole Devine Construction debacle. Dear old Dad can't let it go. He continues to push me toward taking over the business. It's as if he thinks one day I'll wake up and discover building houses is what I want to do with my life. I thought when I made captain, he'd finally give up. But he hasn't."

He exhaled, and a shadow fell over his face when he bowed his head.

The food arrived, giving him the perfect excuse to stop talking.

She had known aspects of Chase's life from many of the conversations she had eavesdropped on, like any self-respecting little sister would do.

She knew all too well what it was like to have a parent who wouldn't listen and didn't understand your hopes and dreams. A parent who pushed their own agenda or interfered.

He interrupted her thoughts a moment later, as if he could read her mind.

"You know you don't have to stay with your mom. I'm sure we could figure something else out for you."

She jotted: *Thanks. But it should be okay.*

Something else? Like where? His place? She could just hear the gossip. And Mom would assume something was going on between them. Well, there was something going on. She just didn't want Mom to know yet. Besides, maybe Mom had changed since Megan left home.

No, she'd stick to her plan. Hopefully, she wouldn't regret this temporary move back to Lucky. Mom could overwhelm Megan even when she was at her best.

❦

Megan rested with her head back and her eyes closed. The melodic "Your Song" by Elton John wafted through the car speakers.

Chase's phone vibrated in the center console, interrupting the peace.

"Are you awake over there?" he whispered. She gave him her thumbs-up sign.

"Can you push the speaker button for me? There's a lot of traffic."

She did as he asked.

"Devine here."

"Chase, honey, it's Char," a woman with a weak, scratchy voice said. It reminded Megan of her Grandma Howard.

"Char." Chase sat up straighter in his seat. He tightened his grip on the wheel, his knuckles whitened. "Is everything all right? Is Tom okay?"

"Well, dear, that's what I'm calling about. I came by the station earlier to speak to you in person, but they told me you wouldn't be back until tomorrow."

"Yeah, that's right. What's going on?"

"Tom has had a slight setback. I hate to ask, but I need to extend my leave. I'm sorry. I know that leaves you in a bind. I could ask my sister—"

"No, Char, I don't want you to give it another thought. You do what you need to do. Take care of Tom. We'll manage. We'll miss you, but we understand."

"Thank you, Chase. I'll stay in touch."

"Please do, Char, and tell Tom I send my get well wishes."

"I will. Thank you," she said.

Megan gave a sideways glance in Chase's direction and saw the consternation on his face. His relaxed demeanor had disappeared.

Finally, he said, "Char works at the station. Char Morgan. She retired from the elementary school about fifteen years ago."

She scribbled a comment on her pad and held it up for him. *She was my first-grade teacher.*

"She's our beloved cook. And I mean Beloved, with a capital B. The guys might cry when I tell them they'll have to eat more of my meatloaf. Who knew cooking could be so hard?" he said, with a halfhearted chuckle.

An idea popped into her head.

She could cook for the guys at the station. She was a good cook, in fact. And it was the least she could do. Chase had done so much for her. She dreaded sitting around Mom's house, doing nothing.

Megan quickly wrote: *I can cook.* She held it up, waving it in front of him.

He didn't take his eyes off the road. "Stop waving that in my face. You'll block my line of vision. And I sure can't read it when you are waving it all around like that."

She complied, holding it still.

He read it. "Okay, so?"

She rolled her eyes at him but at least she had his attention. She scribbled her message again, only this time she printed in all caps, underlined with exclamation marks. She waved it at him. *I CAN COOK!!!*

"Will you please stop waving that in my face?" He pushed it away.

Megan glared and steadied her hand so he could read what she had written.

He began shaking his head immediately. "Absolutely not. No way."

She sighed dramatically. So he'd know he'd made her mad.

"We're not discussing this. It's out of the question. I'm bringing you home to rest and recuperate. Not to wear yourself out cooking for a bunch of men." He pounded the steering wheel for emphasis. "End of subject."

She glared at him.

He laughed. "You can glare all you want, but we're not discussing it. I don't want to hear another word about it."

What a high-handed, bossy attitude. She grabbed her pad, scribbling quickly.

"Yep. And the subject is now closed. Put the pad down, close your eyes, and take another nap. We should be home before seven."

Had he just tried to *handle* her?

Megan turned away and stared out the window. She hid her clenched hands and fumed.

Sleep? He didn't know her at all.

He might have thought it was over, but it was far from over. She'd get the stubborn jerk to cooperate. Or she'd do it her way.

This nonverbal communication was a load of crap. She needed her voice.

Chapter 15

Lucky

An hour and a half later, they pulled into the parking lot in front of Bud's Doggie Day Care. Since it was on the way into town and only a mile down the road from Chase's place, it made sense to get Brady first.

Since Bud was a friend, he didn't have any issue with the after-hours pickup. Then the plan was to drop Brady at Chase's house before he took her home.

His dog charged out with obvious joy at being sprung. He greeted Chase, then saw Megan sitting on a bench in the lobby. He rushed to her side, sniffed, and put his head in her lap. Staring up at her with his sweet brown eyes, he put his right paw up and tapped her lap.

"It looks like he's checking you out to make sure you're okay. Dogs are ultra-sensitive to human feelings. They can sense when we aren't up to par," Chase said.

Up to par. Ha. That was one way to describe her. Megan burrowed her face in Brady's silky fur.

At the house, Brady stood at the door beside Chase, his tail wagging a mile a minute.

They entered through the small laundry room next to the kitchen, and Brady charged past. The dog had completely stolen her heart when she'd stayed last time. But the excited greeting she got from him at the kennel cemented the deal.

Now home, the dog was making his rounds. He sniffed each piece of furniture, located each of his toys, making sure they were where he'd left them. Bemused, she smiled.

Chase must have seen him do it so often, he ignored Brady's inspection. "Ready to go?" he asked her, putting his hand on her back. Warmth penetrated her light blouse. Even with their spat, the man could still make her body tingle with a mere touch.

As if sensing her reluctance, he said, "It'll be all right. Ruby will be over the moon to have you back home. Despite being quite the character, she genuinely cares for you and Kell. She talks about both of you all the time."

Megan dipped her head, and he tipped her chin up with his thumb and stared into her eyes. She thought he was going to kiss her. But the moment passed, and he stepped away.

"Let's go. I need to get you home before Ruby sends out a search party. That woman scares the hell out of me on a good day." He chuckled and started for the door.

"Brady, you be a good boy, and I'll be back in a little while. Go lie down on your bed." He pointed and Brady obeyed, bouncing over to the large dog bed beside the sofa.

Megan wanted to say no. She wasn't ready to go. But she nodded and followed him out the door they'd come through only a few minutes earlier.

Outside, Chase looked between his truck and her car. "Are you up to making the short drive home? I'll follow you in my truck." Before she could answer, he rushed to say, "If you aren't up to it, don't worry about it. I'll drive and get someone from the fire station to run me home."

Megan felt drained of energy because of the painkillers and the lengthy road trip. It felt like someone had mopped the floor with her. Chase noticed and decided for her. He walked to the passenger side of her car and opened the door. "Get in."

She wasn't going to argue.

The man was a paradox. One minute, he was high- handed, controlling, and bossy and the next he was a big mush at the sight of his dog. He was a caring, thoughtful person in more than one way.

Just after he made her so mad, he turns around and does something super sweet.

Megan watched from the front window of the house she grew up in as taillights faded to mere specks. She twisted her hands, and her leg jiggled as if it had a mind of its own. If only Chase hadn't had to get home.

"Too bad we must keep the marriage thing under wraps. Guess we wouldn't want the small-town gossips going crazy if they got wind of it, right?" he'd said on the short drive over.

She didn't know how to respond. What was his point?

She hoped he wouldn't mind too much when she went around him and jumped right into the cooking at the fire station. Because she had every intention of doing just that.

She'd have to think about the best way to go about it. She needed a few more days to rest and get her strength back.

Once the taillights were out of sight, she sighed and turned to Mom. The woman could drive Megan batshit crazy, but she loved her. And it was good to be in the house she grew up in.

Mom must have been asking a question. Megan opened her mouth to reply, then stopped and picked up the pen and notepad. This was getting old. She wrote: *Sorry. What?* She held it up for her mom to read.

"Honey, I asked if you would like some hot tea. Or something else? I made your favorite brownies this afternoon. Or, if you prefer, David and I are having a nightcap. I'm happy to pour one for you, too." She held up a bottle of brandy in her best Vanna White impersonation.

Megan shook her head, and her mother set the bottle down on the makeshift bar in the corner. A recent addition to the living room since Megan had lived here. No way was she going to mix alcohol with her pain meds.

Tea sounds perfect, thanks.

In the kitchen Mom said, "Sit down. I'll make the tea. Sit." When Mom ordered, you obeyed.

Megan feared Mom still saw her as a child, despite all that Megan had accomplished in two short years.

She sat at the kitchen table where she'd sat a hundred of times. She'd done homework, eaten family meals, and played dozens of board and card games here. The kitchen had always been the gathering spot.

Only tonight there was another person, a stranger, sitting at the table, too. Mom's boyfriend. He seemed nice enough. How serious was this relationship? Flavor of the month came to mind. Mom was rarely without male companionship.

But he was still a stranger, and he made Megan uncomfortable. The man had done nothing in particular. But it's normal to feel uneasy around any male stranger after her attack. Right? Megan stood and walked back into the living room and Mom followed.

Megan scribbled on her pad.

Is he leaving soon?

Mom gave her a blank stare. As if she didn't know who Megan was referring to.

Is he staying here tonight?

"Yes, dear. He planned to. Is that a problem?"

Frustration stirred in Megan. Couldn't Mom set aside her libido for one lousy night? Didn't she see that a strange man in the house unnerved Megan?

Megan wrote: *Mom, a man attacked me only a few days ago. Having a male stranger around makes me jittery.*

Mom nibbled her lip. "Oh dear, honey. I'm sorry. But it's David. The man who attacked you is in Tennessee."

David is still a stranger to me.

Why did it seem like Mom was missing a sensitivity chip? Or a little maternal intuition. There was a definite disconnect.

I won't be able to relax. I'm sorry.

She found it frustrating to have to explain and apologize for this.

"All right, darling. We can go to his place."

Megan frowned and shook her head.

I want to be with you, Mom. Just you.

Shit, she felt the tears pooling in her eyes. She did not want to cry. She inhaled and counted to three.

Mom squeezed her hands. "Okay. I'd like to spend time with you, too. I'll talk to David. He's an amiable man. Once you get to know him, you'll see."

Despite her efforts, a few tears leaked. Megan brushed the moisture from her cheeks as the teakettle whistled in the kitchen.

Later, Megan was lying in bed when her phone vibrated on the bedside table, alerting her to an incoming text.

Chase: *Checking on my favorite Nashville star. How are you?*

Megan: *Just peachy.*

The responding text bubbles appeared immediately.

Chase: *Joking aside, how are you feeling? Settled in? And what about Ruby?*

Megan: *The truth?*

Chase: *Nothing but...*

Megan: *I'm okay. Still jumpy. It's kind of gross watching Mom make googly eyes at her boyfriend. (Throwing up emoji).*

Chase: *(Smiling devil emoji).*

Megan: *(Eye roll emoji). I'm feeling jittery around him.*

Chase: *That's understandable.*

Megan: *I feel bad. He seems to like her.*

Chase: *Give yourself time.*

Megan: *Yeah. Guess I have to. Thanks again for bringing me home.*

Two weeks after arriving in Lucky, Megan had her first appointment with the otolaryngologist at the Cleveland Clinic.

She rode shotgun as her mom drove them home afterward. She watched as the world flew past, lost in her thoughts.

At least the doctor had given her permission to use her voice again, as long as she didn't raise it. And it was raspy. But Megan was relieved to put the notepad and pen away.

"Honey, did you hear what I said? Are you even listening to me?" Mom asked.

She shook her head. "Sorry, what did you say?"

"I asked what the doctor said."

"He's *cautiously* optimistic." Megan air quoted the word. Her singing voice might never recover to the level it had been before the incident. Hopefully, the operative word was *might*. The doctor wasn't willing to guarantee anything yet.

"It wasn't terrible news. My speaking voice is back if I don't strain. I'll continue to sound raspy for a while still." She shrugged. "Aren't raspy voices supposed to be sexy? I just sound like I smoke three-packs-a-day." She forced a laugh. "At least I have no more pain when I swallow."

"That's awesome news, honey." But then, out of left field, her mother asked, "Is he handsome?"

"Who?" Where had that question come from?

"The doctor. Is he good-looking?"

"Mom. You can't be serious."

"Of course I am. You always need to keep an eye out for husband material."

If she only knew.

"There is so much wrong with that statement, I don't know what to say. Let's stay focused here. I'm not looking for husband material. I want to recover my singing voice so I can get back to my career."

"It never hurts to keep — "

She held her hand up. "Mom. Stop." From the expression on Mom's face, it was clear Megan had hurt her feelings. Sad eyes and a pouty lip were not an attractive look on a woman in her fifties.

"Mom, can we just stay focused on my recovery? Then we'll worry about finding me a husband. How does that sound?"

Mom only nodded.

Thank God they were nearly back to Lucky.

For the next week, Megan hung out with Mom. Tucked under a light blanket on the sofa, they talked and reminisced. When Mom was in her pampering mode, she knew how to make someone feel good. Megan felt stronger every day.

Although Mom doted on her during the day, she spent the evenings out. Megan assumed at David's place. Megan was restless in the quiet house, especially after dark. She hated to admit that every creak spooked her.

Was it better to have David there at night than being in the lonely, creepy house? As it turned out, she didn't need to bring it up. One evening, David came for supper and stayed overnight. She guessed the logic being that by now Megan had gotten to know David.

That was true enough.

Chapter 16

Megan was running. Running for her life. She struggled for breath. Her heart pounded. Her chest hurt. Fear pulsed through her body.

His feet pounded the ground behind her.

Thump. Thump. Thump.

He was closing in on her.

Closer.

He grabbed her from behind, pulling her against his hard body. She screamed. But there was no sound. She had no voice.

He slammed her against the wall.

Wham. Wham. Wham.

Megan woke with a start, gulping for air. Her body, drenched in sweat, shook uncontrollably. She tried to slow her breathing so she wouldn't hyperventilate. She shoved the sheets down so she could sit on the edge of the bed.

Deep breaths.

She shook her head. *It was only a bad dream.* Yeah, tell that to her erratic heartbeat and racing pulse. It had felt so real. She was back in Nashville and Jason caught her. Ge slammed her against the car. Over and over.

She continued to work on her breathing, calming her body. God, she needed to get back to yoga. She reached to turn on the bedside lamp, but it took a few tries with her clammy, shaky hand.

She blinked. The little clock showed it was one o'clock.

Sighing, she took a sip of the water she always kept beside the bed at night.

Calmer, she flipped her pillow over and lay her cheek on the cool side as she pulled up the blanket. She let out a breath, and her eyelids drooped.

Wham. Wham. Wham.

She bolted upright. The noise was real. It was not part of that nightmare. The banging came from the wall behind her bed. It sounded like the bed was getting jammed up against the wall, like during sex.

Ew. Gross. Really, Mom?

When the banging finally stopped, she shook the images from her mind.

Punching her pillow, Megan laid back down, closing her eyes, just drifting off....

Thump. Thump. Thump.

"Oh. My. God. You've got to be kidding," she muttered to herself.

The framed picture that hung on the wall over Megan's bed jiggled with each thump. Now that her attention was hyper-focused, she heard more sounds through the thin walls. The extra noises corresponded with the wall-banging. Was that moaning?

She put her hands over her ears and sang la, la, la in her head. And while she may have been able to block the sounds, the images in her mind's eye were permanent.

Not that her mom was too old to be having sex. She would be only fifty-three on her next birthday. She still had whatever attracted men.

Megan finally threw off the covers and stomped down the hall to Kell's bedroom. It was the farthest bedroom away from Ruby's Red Room. Megan prayed it was far enough.

Shit. Kell's room didn't look like it had seen a dust cloth in ages. Boxes stacked on the floor and on his bed cluttered the space. It would take her hours to get the room reorganized so she could sleep in the bed.

She was too exhausted. She considered crawling over the boxes to wedge herself against the wall, but decided against the middle-of-the-night aerobic exercise. Megan was marching back to her room when her phone buzzed with a text.

Chase: *Passed your house on the way back to the station. Light on in Kell's room. Everything okay?*

Megan: *Yep. Can't sleep.*

Chase: What are you doing in your bro's room at this time of night?

Megan: Trying to escape the wall-banging sex happening in Ruby's red room.

He didn't respond right away.

Megan: Well, don't you have anything snappy to say?

Chase: *Go Ruby? (Thumbs-up emoji).*

> Megan: *Ha, ha. Funny. Oh, never mind. I'm using my earbuds.*

> Chase: *Good plan. G'night.*

> Megan: *Night.*

She smiled. Chase had that innate ability to calm her down. If David was going to be staying overnight every night, Megan figured three was definitely a crowd. It would not work. She wondered if either of the two inns in Lucky had vacancies. Where could she stay where she'd feel safe?

As she lay there, now wide awake—thanks, Mom, and David—she hatched a two-part plan. Despite it being the middle of the night, she sent a text for Brenda to see first thing in the morning. It took more than a beep or phone vibration to wake her.

> Megan: *I know it's earlier than what we talked about, but can you bring Emmie up?*

> *Pretty please. I need my sweet girl and I wouldn't mind seeing your smiling face either. (Smile emoji).*

With part one of her plan in motion, she rolled over and tried to sleep. She still laid awake, but it was no longer because of her mother's sexual escapades in the next room. She lay awake picturing her own wall-banging experience with Chase in Las Vegas.

For the hundredth time, she cursed the fact that she still couldn't recall their night in Vegas. It was more of a feeling or sense she got about their time together. She knew without a doubt that he'd rocked her world even though she couldn't remember the small but important details.

The next morning, she craved coffee to help wake up. But she sipped her herbal tea with honey. She was contemplating the best way to tell Mom she was moving out when her phone vibrated with a text.

Brenda: *Got your message. Booked on the noon flight. Tomorrow. Should I rent a car? (Heart emoji).*

Megan: *Thank you. Not unless you want a car. I'm happy to pick you up. And you can use my car while you're here. Love you. (Heart emoji).*

Brenda: *I'd love for you to get me. I'll send the flight details later.*

Megan: *(Heart and smiley emoji)*

Part one was underway, but now she had to face Mom. That was a whole other matter. Sighing, she braced for an argument.

Mom walked into the room. "Good morning." She took the seat next to Megan. "Sweetie, you look tired. Didn't you sleep well?"

"No, not really."

Megan felt her face heat with embarrassment. This wasn't something she wanted to talk about with her mother. But she wasn't a teenager. She could do it.

"What? I'm sorry. Do we need to replace your old mattress?"

"The mattress was fine."

"Did the bed squeak too much?"

Well, she was getting warmer. She couldn't go through the torture of twenty questions.

She blurted, "You and David made a lot of noise last night and woke me up. And I couldn't fall back asleep."

Now it was her mother's turn to blush. "For heaven's sake, you're a grown woman. Sex is perfectly natural."

Megan set her teacup on the saucer with a clatter and leaned her elbows on the table to get closer to her mother. "True, but I still don't want to hear my mother moaning through the wall."

Mom thought for a moment, then said, "I suppose David and I can be more discreet or stay at his place. It can be difficult because he has teenagers off and on. He shares custody with his ex."

Megan shook her head. "This is your house. I don't want you to feel you have to leave because of me. Besides, I found another place to stay. I'm moving there this morning."

Her mom's eyes widened. "What?" Megan held up her hand.

"Plus, I miss Emmie. Brenda is flying in tomorrow with my baby. Think of her as my therapy cat. With your allergy to cats, I can't have her in your house."

Mom's eyes widened.

"Remember the health scare we had when I was ten and snuck that cute little black kitten into the house?"

"You cried for days. I wasn't sure it was for me or losing the kitten," said Mom.

Megan smiled. "A little of both, I think."

"But do you have to leave? Can't we think of another arrangement?"

"No, I'd worry about your health."

Mom frowned, but finally agreed. "I guess you're right."

Megan smiled, patting her mother on the arm.

"Where will you stay?"

Megan took a deep breath, praying that part two of her hatched plan worked out with as much ease as the first part. "I'm staying at Chase's place. He's got a guest room."

"Chase?" her mom said. "Are you serious? What will people think?"

Megan shrugged. "I don't care."

"Sounds like you have it all thought out, and he has always looked after you. It makes sense."

But what if he says no? What if he says yes?

Megan bit her lip, cursed her doubtful thoughts.

What would happen to their friendship if they got together? Would they be jeopardizing their relationship? She wasn't saying anything would happen between them, but what if...

Sucking in a deep breath, she exhaled.

Put your big girl Nikes on. Just do it.

Chapter 17

The sound of the doorbell woke Chase. "Go away."

The bell rang a second time, and he threw off his covers. "This better be important." It was Sunday and Chase had the day off. He snatched his T-shirt from the chair in the corner of his bedroom. "What are you so happy about?" he grumbled to Brady.

The dog trailed closely behind Chase, confident that whoever was at the door had come to play. Brady's tail wagged with happiness, unbothered by the early hour.

The bell rang a third time as Chase reached the door. "Brady, go lie down," he commanded. He pulled his shirt on as he opened the door. "Hold your damn horses," he growled.

He blinked. Was he dreaming? Megan stood on his porch, bouncing from foot to foot with her arms wrapped around her waist, and he immediately wanted to take back his grumbling.

"Oh my God, did I interrupt something? Is it too early? I'm sorry. I should have call—." She covered her face with her hands.

He pulled her hands down. "You haven't."

"Are you sure?"

A loud guffaw escaped. "I'm pretty sure I would know if you interrupted anything."

She ignored his remark as if she hadn't heard him.

"It's Sunday morning. I should have considered you could have someone here." She ran her hand through her mass of unruly curls.

"Stop. Take a breath. No one is here. No one was here. It's only Brady and me."

The darkness under her eyes stood out on her pale face. She looked beat.

"What's wrong?" He pulled her into his arms.

With her head tucked into his chest, he had trouble understanding her muffled words. He reluctantly let her go. "What?"

"I'm fine, tired, but fine," she whispered. Her voice sounded stronger, but still raspy. The raspy tone was sexy as hell.

The real Megan was so much hotter than the version who visited his dreams. Even in her current ashen, tired state, she was a welcome sight.

"Come in." He put his arm around her back and pushed her through the doorway. His eyes narrowed. "What are you doing here? This early, I mean. As I recall, you love to sleep in."

Before she could respond, Brady galloped over to her, his tail wagging like crazy.

"Who's a good boy? Brady's a good boy," she whispered, as she patted his head.

"Brady, I told you to go lie down."

"If it's okay, I don't mind at all."

"Okay by me. Want coffee?"

She shook her head. "Do you have any tea?"

"I'll check. Might be old. I stock it for Mom. It's been a while since she visited."

Thank God for programmable coffeemakers. He poured himself a cup, then he found the box of tea in his cupboard and held it up. "Mint?"

"That's fine."

He found the tea kettle hidden behind his pots and pans.

While he prepared her tea, he watched her fidget. Her brow furrowed, and she twisted her hands. He set her mug on the counter beside her. "What's going on, Megan? Would you like me to find paper and a pen? Are you sure you should use your voice?"

"The Doc says as long as I don't strain, it's okay."

He nodded.

Circling back, he said, "How could you think there'd be someone here overnight with me? I'm a married man." He grinned and winked, hoping his tease would hit the mark and help her relax. "Now drink your tea."

As if on cue, Brady maneuvered around Chase and plowed his nose right into Megan's crotch.

"Brady, no," Chase said, reaching for the dog's collar.

Giggling, Megan crouched down so she was on Brady's level. She scratched behind his ears and kissed his furry head.

"It's official. I'm jealous of my dog. Brady, please leave Megan alone." He clapped his hands, and Brady stopped and looked up at Chase with his sad brown eyes.

"Good boy. Go lie down." He pointed to the living room. Then turned his attention back to Megan. "Now, sit down and ignore my star-struck dog. Want anything else? Toast? Eggs? Some juice?" He opened the fridge. "Looks like I have cranberry or V-8." He turned in time to see her eye roll. "What's with the somersaulting eyes?"

"Nothing. You're just such a guy."

"Last time I checked."

"Ha. It's just that you and Kell are so much alike. He loves V-8, too." She cocked her head. "Or at least he used to. He's been gone so long, it's hard to know what he likes," Megan said wistfully.

"It's good. You should try it sometime. A blend of eight vegetables, yada yada."

She turned her nose up, and he grinned. "I'll just drink my tea, thank you."

He poured himself a V-8, sat down across from her, took a drink, and made an exaggerated ahhh. "Could've had a V-8."

She laughed, "You're a riot."

"You sound better," he said.

She fidgeted in her seat again.

"So, what's up? Are you ready to talk about brought you over here so early this morning?"

Megan chewed on her lower lip. He waited. She was unusually nervous, which was out of character for her. She stood and paced the length of his kitchen. He continued to wait. She had to be working up to something.

"So, um, I was thinking... I have a proposition."

"Oh, yeah?" He waggled his eyebrows suggestively. "Do tell. Am I going to like this proposition?"

She punched his arm. "I mean, what I'm trying to ask is, would it be okay if I stayed here with you instead of at my mom's place?"

His eyes widened. He wasn't expecting that.

She rushed on. "It's Mom and David, the boyfriend, and the whole wall-banging sex thing. It's loud. And I don't see them stopping on account of her adult daughter in the next room." She took a deep breath. "I'm exhausted. I didn't sleep at all."

That explained some things.

"That bad?"

She nodded. "Worse."

"Yikes."

"Yes, yikes, and I'll raise you an ew." Her face wrinkled in mock disgust.

He shivered and shook his head to dislodge the image of Ruby getting busy with anyone. "Are you sure?"

"Oh my God, Chase, of course I'm sure the wall shook. Wham. Wham. Wham." She slammed her hand on the counter, punctuating her point. Brady came rushing into the kitchen to check out the noise.

Chase placed his hands over hers. "Stop. I get the awkward picture, unfortunately. I meant, are you sure you want to move in here? How are we going to explain it? Might get complicated."

"I have that all figured out." She rubbed her hands together as she sat back down at his kitchen table.

"Sounds like you've given it some thought."

She scoffed. "Are you kidding? I had all night to think."

He motioned for her to continue.

"First, I explained to Mom that I could hear their nocturnal activities through the thin wall. Talk about awkward. You can imagine how embarrassing it would be to discuss your parents' sex life."

He shook his head, motioning with his hand for her to move on. "Nope, not going there."

"It's her house—and if she wants to have hours and hours and hours of sex, that's her business." She cringed. "I don't want to listen in. Thank you very much."

"Okay. Go on." "So I told her I was moving in with you." He nodded. "And what did your mom say about the new living arrangements? No way do I want the wrath of Ruby coming down on me."

"Coward," she teased.

"You bet your sweet ass. Ruby Howard is Scary, with a capital S."

"You don't need to worry. She understands. She can't be around a cat."

"As far as I can see, there's only one problem with that plan. Emmie isn't here."

She tapped her head with her index finger. "Thought of that." Grinning, she continued, "Brenda is flying up with her. They will be here tomorrow."

He blinked. Had to give her points for cleverness.

"Do you accept my proposition? I promise to be on my best behavior."

He wanted to ask her what she considered her best behavior to be.

Hell, she wanted to move in and spend the rest of her time in Lucky at his place. He wanted to fist bump the air. Of course she could move in. She could stay for as long as she liked.

Forever.

Trying for nonchalance, he asked, "What about Brady and Emmie? Do you think they'll get along?"

She was nibbling on her lower lip again. "Hmm, I hadn't thought about that part. But Brady is a sweetheart. Do you think he'll mind sharing his house with Emmie?"

"He'll be fine with it. There are a couple of cats at the doggie daycare, pets of the owner. Occasionally, the cats escape the house and pay a visit to the kennels. Brady seems to get along with everyone."

Brady wagged his tail when he heard his name. He spotted a fluorescent yellow tennis ball, and like a heat-seeking missile, he zoomed to it and plopped his prize at Megan's feet.

Chased laughed. "Good boy." He grabbed the ball and tossed it. "Looks like Brady is onboard."

"Guess it's settled then." She grinned.

"Guess so. When you're ready, we can head over to get your stuff."

"Actually, my bags are in the car." He arched a brow. "Pretty sure of yourself."

She shrugged with a crooked smile. "More like desperate and hopeful." He squeezed her hand. "I'll go grab your gear. You can have a seat in the other room and get better acquainted with your new roomie." But she didn't move. He added, "Unless you want to supervise?"

She shook her head.

"I'll bring everything up to the guest room where you stayed the last time."

As he passed her, she reached out and squeezed his arm. He tensed, silently begging his body not to react to her touch.

"Thanks. This means a lot to me. You're my real-life hero."

Unable to speak, he nodded and walked out of the room. If only she knew how much he wanted it to be true. It appeared she had forgiven him—now if only he could forgive himself.

He made several trips in and out of the house, hauling her things up the stairs to the bedroom. Afterward, he walked back into the kitchen for a second cup of coffee.

It was ironic that Megan had seemed so nervous to ask to stay with him. Because if he were honest, he loved the idea and was thrilled with this development. For her own good, of course. He could protect her better if she was near. Purely altruistic.

You're so full of shit.

Chapter 18

Brenda came through the airport gate area with the cat carrier in hand, and Megan breathed a sigh of relief.

She had missed Emmie so much. Seeing Brenda relaxed her, too. She was like family, the kind you got along with and who didn't get on your very last nerve.

Megan was very certain that her decision to stay with Chase was the right one. Hopefully, Chase was happy, too. Only time would tell.

He was such a sweetheart to invite Brenda to stay at the house instead of one of the bed-and-breakfast places in town. It would give the two women a chance to spend more time together.

And any worries that Brady wouldn't share his humble abode with a feline vanished as soon as he saw the cat. He welcomed Emmie as he did any newcomer. Sniffed. Fetched his ball, almost dropping it on her head, clearly wanting her to play a friendly game of catch.

But Emmie scampered under the sofa. She'd never been around other animals except on her vet visits, and then she was in her protective carrier. Once Emmie was brave enough to come out from under the furniture, it seemed like they had come to a tacit agreement to get along.

Megan slept soundly that night. Perhaps because she hadn't gotten much sleep, the few nights before or because Emmie cuddled up on the pillow beside her. It might have been the fact that Brenda had arrived or knowing that Chase was close by if she needed him. Whatever the reason, she felt rested the next day.

During Brenda's two-week stay, the two friends kept busy, and Megan could relax more each day. Brenda got to meet the small support group Megan had connected with—women who had been victims of a crime.

And she even talked Brenda into going with her to the first self-defense class she'd enrolled in. It was so comforting to have her best friend along to do things with, especially when Chase was at work.

Megan hated the idea of sitting around and feeling sorry for herself. Worse was the fear that Jason still loomed at large. No arrest yet.

By the time the two weeks were up, her bruising had all but faded, and Megan felt like her old self.

The night before Brenda's early morning flight back to Nashville, Megan invited her mom and David to join them at Joe's for a farewell dinner. Everything was going fine until Megan shared she had another appointment with Dr. Hartley, the specialist in Cleveland, the following week.

"Oh, Megan, honey, that's wonderful. Maybe this time you can find out if he's married."

"What?" She snuck a quick peek at Chase across the table. He and Brenda had been chatting. But their talk ended at the precise moment Mom made her ridiculous comment.

Chase's blank expression gave away nothing, but Brenda's eyes widened.

"What difference does that make?" Megan asked.

"A single young woman your age should always pay attention to that detail," Mom said, as if it were the most practical thing in the world.

"It doesn't matter. I'm not dating him. I'm seeing him about my larynx. I'm his patient."

"I know that. But it never hurts to be prepared."

"Mom."

"It's not like there are many eligible guys here in Lucky."

Embarrassed, Megan blushed. Now Chase was frowning.

"That's rude. Chase is sitting right here. He's an eligible man. There are lots of men. Not that it matters. I'm not looking for a date—I'm looking for help so I can save my singing voice. And my career."

She turned to Chase and mouthed, "Sorry."

He shrugged.

"I'm just trying to help you, dear. What are you planning to wear?"

Thank goodness their food arrived in time for Mom to miss everyone's uncomfortable faces. She had a one-track mind with men as the ultimate destination.

Hopefully, Chase brushed it off.

After dropping Brenda off at the airport, Chase took Brady for a morning walk, which left Megan alone in the house.

She wandered into the room that Brenda had been using. Typical of her friend, Brenda had already tidied up, and the bedding lay piled, ready for a trip to the laundry room.

It sure was quiet. No close neighbors. A shiver ran down Megan's spine.

Stop that, she chided herself. There was no reason to be afraid, but she still couldn't help but think about how it would be when Chase worked a forty-eight-hour shift.

Megan hated the fear. It made her feel weak. She was sitting on the edge of the sofa when she heard Chase come back inside.

"Megan?" he shouted from the kitchen, already moving into the living room.

"In here," she whispered.

"Hey, are you okay?"

She nodded. "Yeah."

"You sure? You don't look okay. Missing Brenda already?"

She gave him a tentative smile. "Yeah, but I guess I was thinking about how vulnerable we are out here. No neighbors." She shivered again. She folded her arms together and rubbed her forearms.

Chase sat beside her. "You're safe here. I'll make sure of it."

"What about when you're on shift?"

He thought for a moment. "If you aren't completely comfortable, we'll think of something. Maybe you can invite your mom for a sleepover?" He grinned.

"You're so NOT funny." She laughed despite her unease. "I'm sorry about what Mom said last night."

"Don't sweat it. I've been around your mom for years. Nothing she says or does can surprise me."

She cocked her head. "True story."

Turning serious, he asked, "You gonna be okay?"

"I think so." She stood. "Hey, can we do something this afternoon? Get out of here for a while, just the two of us?"

"Sure. Where'd you like to go?"

"Hmm." She glanced out her window at the sun glistening off the lake. "How about we take a picnic out on the boat?"

"I'm good with that."

"Great. Soaking up some sunshine and a swim will be just the ticket."

Chase was just drifting off to sleep when there was a noise in the hall. It wasn't Brady, since he was asleep on his comfy bed in the corner. Figuring it had to be Megan, he watched as she poked her head into the room.

She took a few hesitant steps, then tiptoed over to the bed. She was reaching down to nudge him when he sat up and asked, "Can't sleep?"

She yelped, and her hand flew to her chest. "Oh my God, Chase, you scared me to death."

He laughed. "I'm not the one creeping into someone's room in the middle of the night."

"It isn't the middle of the night. You went to bed like fifteen minutes ago, and I wasn't creeping. I was tiptoeing. I didn't want to scare you."

Having Megan in his bedroom, standing so close to his bed was doing things to his body that he'd rather she not notice.

"What do you need, Megan?" Chase didn't mean to sound brusque. But he could smell her sweet fragrance. And the T-shirt and shorts she wore should have done nothing to entice him, but on her it was sexy as hell. He found it difficult to hide his reaction.

"I'm wondering if I could maybe lie down next to you."

She sounded so young and vulnerable, it about broke his heart.

He patted the bed. "What's going on?"

She twisted her hands in her lap. "I'm sorry to be a bother."

He took her hands in his to stop her fidgeting. "You're not a bother. What's going on?"

He let go of her hands long enough to switch on the bedside light. It was a low- wattage bulb, so it gave him enough light to see her face but didn't blind the two of them.

"It's—she took a deep breath and exhaled—"when I close my eyes, I keep seeing Jason." She shivered.

He wrapped an arm around her. "Have you been having trouble sleeping every night?" He couldn't believe he'd missed her sleeplessness.

"No, actually, I slept fine while Brenda was here. I guess with everything we did, exhaustion helped. Plus, she and I stayed up some nights and talked for hours."

He nodded. Then another thought occurred to him. "You aren't nervous about being here alone with me, are you?" He pulled back so he could see her face.

"Not at all. Maybe it's just tonight. I don't know."

It was obvious she needed reassurance. "You can sleep here." He stood; glad he wore shorts to bed. "Get under the covers, and I'll sleep on top."

"Are you sure?"

He nodded. "Come on. Climb in." He held the covers up for her to slide in.

She settled into the spot where he had been, and he grabbed a throw off the chair in the corner and joined her.

It wasn't long before her body sagged, relaxing into him with the slow, even breathing of sleep. It was only then that he closed his own eyes.

Chapter 19

Somewhere off the grid…

Holed up in an Indiana motel room, Jason sorted through what remained of his Megan photos and souvenirs. It was too bad that he couldn't bring more of the photos from the montage in his apartment. It was a pittance of his collection, which he assumed was now confiscated by the police. It probably sat unappreciated in some evidence locker.

He'd have to be satisfied with the photos and videos he'd saved on the laptop.

Escaping Nashville had been a piece of cake. He'd withdrawn all his money from the bank and ditched his credit cards months ago.

Good thing.

Stealing a neighbor's car had been easy, then he'd switched the plates with a car he found in a Walmart lot north of Nashville. He'd repeated the process outside of Louisville.

He'd been driving the back roads of Kentucky and Indiana for several hours. Now he wanted to relax by watching a Megan video.

They must have found his camera because the feed in her bedroom was dead. He wasn't surprised. Not that he gave the cops much credit. It wouldn't take an Einstein to connect the dots.

Anyone could see she was in her bedroom when several of the photos were taken. The angle and quality screamed *hidden camera*. Now the cops could see they weren't dealing with some third-rate idiot. His abilities on a computer were superior, and there was nothing he could not access or replicate.

So he settled back on the bed to watch Megan reruns on his laptop. He clicked on one of his favorite videos and watched as she undressed, then sat on the edge of her bed while she put on lotion.

He'd stay put a little longer. It wasn't like he had to be in a hurry. He had all the time in the world and wanted to make sure his plan was perfect. He needed a course of action. But there was no doubt in his mind, Megan was going to pay for uprooting his life.

Chapter 20

Two days later, Megan set her alarm early enough to get to the fire station in time to fix breakfast. Chase's stubborn directive that she couldn't cook for the men would not stop her. She could be just as stubborn as him. She'd blame her Scottish ancestry and auburn hair.

She needed something to do. Something to focus on other than herself and her problems and fears. With Brenda gone and Chase working, the house felt empty—even with two four-legged companions.

Besides, she owed Chase more than before. Making breakfast was a simple way to pay him back for letting her move in. And he had shown her such kindness when she couldn't sleep the night Brenda left.

But if he didn't like her plan, he could just stick his mad where the sun didn't shine.

As soon as she got into the firehouse kitchen, she checked to see that the coffeemaker was set to start soon. Good. She laid out the groceries she'd picked up the day before on the counter and got to work. She scrambled two dozen eggs and set them aside to cook once the men woke up and were ready to eat.

Bacon and sausage were next on her list. The familiar savory smells of breakfast soon wafted through the whole place.

Two men stumbled into the kitchen, rubbing sleep from their eyes. They both stared and blinked, as if she were a mirage.

She smiled and waved. "Morning, guys."

"Morning," they mumbled in unison.

Maybe Chase hadn't mentioned her being in town.

If he had, hopefully, he didn't mention why. She no longer wore the bandage on her forehead. Nothing a little makeup couldn't hide.

"Coffee is ready. Help yourselves," she said. "I've got scrambled eggs ready to cook if you'd like some. Bacon and sausage, too."

She chuckled at their expressions—a mixture of bafflement, gratitude, and glee.

One of men, the older of the two, spoke up, "Umm, we have mess duty this morning."

"Then it's your lucky day, because I'm cooking for you."

"For real?" asked the younger man.

"For real." She laughed at his obvious joy.

"Does the Captain—"

She brushed her hands on the apron she'd donned. "Hi. I'm Megan. I'm staying with Chase ...er, Captain Devine." She bit her lip to keep from laughing. Captain Devine sounded like a superhero or a male stripper.

"Anyway, I heard you lost your cook for a while. I thought I'd make myself useful while I'm in town and help around here."

The two men were nodding like twin bobbleheads. It looked like they were about to open their mouths to say something when Chase's raised voice came from outside the door.

"Michaels, Ross, smells like you got breakfast started." He turned the corner and stopped short. Megan was at the stove.

Chase's good humor evaporated like rain on hot cement. His two rookies spoke up before he could get a word out.

"We had nothing to do with this."

"We were as surprised as you."

Knowing Megan as he did, Chase had no doubt that was exactly what happened. "Don't worry about it." He smiled. "Looks like we have ourselves a delicious breakfast to enjoy. But you two are on KP cleanup."

Michaels and Ross both nodded and answered in unison, "Yes, sir."

Megan had busied herself as soon as he'd walked into the kitchen, but he wasn't about to let her get away with this. "Megan, I'd like a word with you. In my office. Now."

"Yes, sir," she said. "Hey, guys, I'll be back in a few minutes."

"After you." He waved his arm in the direction of his office. "Third door on the right." Her ponytail swung back and forth as she marched down the hall.

His gaze traveled downward and settled on her ass seconds before they reached his office. He raised his gaze and closed the door.

"Take a seat," he said.

"No, thanks. I prefer to take my dressing down standing up." She gave him one of her fake smiles. She had no idea that her sass drove him crazy. "This can't take long, or the food will burn."

Fine. They'd stand. "What the hell are you doing here?"

"What does it look like I'm doing?"

"It looks like you did exactly what I told you not to do."

"At the risk of sounding like a child, you aren't the boss of me," she said, sticking out her tongue.

That's mature.

He scrubbed at the whiskers on his jawline. "No, but I am the boss here." He frowned.

"If you're done yelling at me, I need to get back to the kitchen to fix more eggs."

"This isn't over. We'll discuss it later."

"Yes, sir, Captain." She saluted before she opened his door and marched back to the kitchen. He heard her call to the group of firefighters who had congregated in the kitchen, "Okay, men, line up, grab a plate, and I'll dish it up."

☘

Later, he sat at his desk, grumbling to himself.

Perhaps if he'd made it clear that he was worried about her doing too much too soon, she'd have responded better. He was concerned for her, wanted her to rest and recuperate.

Getting up early to cook breakfast for a bunch of men didn't align with rest and recovery, in his mind.

She'd never intended to follow his order. She was still as ornery as she'd been when she used to trail behind Kell and him when they were desperate to ditch her.

Why would she listen now? She had been a handful as a child. Ruby used to call her strong-willed. Bullshit—she was plain old bull-headed.

He was still complaining to himself when Megan knocked on his open door. She carried a steaming cup of coffee and a plate overflowing with breakfast food.

"Permission to enter, Captain." With a smirk on her face, she handed him the cup and plate. "Here, grumpy pants."

Begrudgingly, he took them and muttered his thanks.

"Now was that so hard?"

"Don't start." He glared at her over the mug. "What am I going to do with you?"

Her eyes sparkled. "Hmm, not sure. But I bet you could come up with a few ideas." She fluttered her eyelashes.

If she was shooting for sexy and seductive, she failed. Instead, it was silly and cute. She still wore the food-stained apron, and her ponytail was now lopsided. She must have sweated off her makeup because her freckles stood out.

He'd been doing a good job of ignoring his feelings for her. But when she flirted and said shit like that, it was all he could do not to kiss her.

So far, he'd been able to keep his hands to himself.

First, Brenda had been around, and now with him on shift, he was safe from the temptation. At least until she showed up at the fire station this morning. He could only hold off for so long. If she kept up with the mischievous innuendos, he was sure to slip.

That couldn't happen. He had to keep telling himself she was under his protection. She was recuperating from a traumatic attack; she needed time.

He'd been mad and frustrated when he realized she'd gone behind his back. But how could he hold on to those emotions? What she had done was sweet and generous. And his men appreciated and deserved a good home-cooked meal during their shifts.

He took a bite of his scrambled eggs. Oh, wow, the best scrambled eggs he'd ever tasted. "These are great. What's your secret?"

"It's just that—a secret. If I tell you, it won't be a secret any longer and you won't need me." She winked.

Oh, he needed her, all right.

The food sure beat what they'd been eating since Char left. No more runny undercooked or tough overcooked eggs. Appetizing aromas replaced the smell of burnt toast.

He shook his head. "You know you've made it impossible for us to enjoy our meals once you leave. At least until Char gets back."

She sat across from him. "I'll do it until I head back to Nashville." She must have recognized his indecision, because she rushed on to say, "I don't mind helping here. Cooking comes easy, and it relaxes me. I'll go crazy sitting around the house all day." She ducked her head, whispering, "Thoughts of Jason creep into my head when I'm idle." Her voice hitched. "And I don't want to think about the possible lasting damage he caused to my vocal cords, at least not yet."

For a moment, it looked like she might cry. Who could blame her? She'd been through so much.

"You're doing me a huge favor letting me crash at your place. It's the least I can do. It's a win-win."

Chase chuckled. "Okay, okay, but we will be on cleanup duty. Cooking the meals is one thing, cleaning the kitchen is another. We'll take care of that." He stood and moved to the front of his desk. "Agreed?"

"Agreed. It's a deal." She stood and extended her hand. But before he shook it, she moved in quickly, kissing him on the lips. She drew back, her eyes wide.

Seconds ticked by while they stared at each other.

Suddenly, he kicked the door shut with one foot and leaned on the edge of his desk. He pulled her to him until she was practically in his lap. Then he kissed her. Light at first, teasing her lips.

She moved her hands from his chest to his shoulders and pulled him even closer. He deepened the kiss, using his tongue to explore her mouth.

Both ignored the window in the door until Michaels strolled past. The probie whistled, and Megan drew back. *Busted.*

Chase frowned at the obvious whisker burn on her cheeks.

She rushed out of his office. *Damn.*

It was time to show her how he felt about her. Dancing around each other, flirting then withdrawing to a safe distance was making him crazy. She hadn't mentioned their marriage, and that was fine with him ... for now. But eventually, they'd need to discuss it and find a solution.

Chapter 21

After his shift ended that afternoon, Chase came through the garage door juggling his duffle and a bouquet of daisies. He'd been wrong to come down so hard on her at the station that morning. Flowers, he hoped, would be the perfect way to apologize. She was only trying to help.

He dropped his duffle in the mudroom next to the washer. It had been a shitty end to his shift.

The O'Donnells' barn fire had taken hours to put out, and they had to call in crews from surrounding counties.

He needed a beer, a hot shower, and his bed. In no special order. But first, he had an apology to make.

He stopped in the kitchen doorway and smiled. His kitchen had never smelled so good. Megan had her back to him, cooking and singing.

She wasn't belting the song, and her voice might not be 100 percent yet, but she was singing, and it was music to his ears. She sounded sexy as hell. The raspy tone wrapped around his dick and pulled.

She bopped to the beat as she stirred whatever was on the stove. Bending, she checked something in the oven. He watched her ass bop to the beat.

His priorities shifted. All he cared about was being right here, right now. Forget the beer, shower, and bed. He leaned against the wall, crossing his legs at his ankles. He set the bouquet on the edge of the counter and shoved his hands into the pockets of his jeans.

Megan, her hips swaying as she used the spatula as a microphone, was singing along to Carrie Underwood's "Last Name." The parallels to their Vegas night slammed into him. Coincidence? Getting drunk and waking up married...

Megan swirled. When she saw Chase leaning against the counter, she dropped the spatula, and her hand flew to her chest as she squealed. "Shit. You scared me half to death." She tapped her phone, and the music stopped.

It would have been humorous if not for the panic on her pale face.

He took his hands out of his pockets and rushed over to her. "Hey, hey, relax. You're safe. I'm sorry. I couldn't resist enjoying the show."

She belted him in the gut. "You should have made yourself known."

"I see that now."

Chase picked up the dropped spatula and tossed it in the sink. He grabbed a paper towel and wiped up the small spill.

She had turned her back to him and sagged against the counter. Her body shook.

Turning her around so he could look her in the eye, he said, "I'm sorry, Megan. That was completely insensitive of me. I should have realized having a man, any man, watching you would creep you out. I'm an idiot."

She was healing so well and adjusting to life here in Lucky, he sometimes let the tragedy drift to the back of his mind. Not cool. She needed him to take better care.

He pulled her into his chest. She sighed and looked up at him. "No, you aren't. This is your house, your kitchen."

He began to interrupt, but she held up her hand. "No, let me finish, please. I need to put the attack behind me. I want you to know I trust you. I feel safe with you."

He nodded. Letting her go, he stepped back and retrieved the flowers.

"These are for you. I want to apologize for my behavior this morning. I acted like a real jerk at the fire station."

"Oh, Chase, this is so sweet. I love daisies. Thank you." Megan smiled. "And no apology needed. I should have asked."

"You did ask."

"Oh, yeah, I did, didn't I?" Grinning, she arched a brow.

He laughed. "So, what's all this?" He waved his arm to indicate the food prep spread out on the counter and cooking in both the oven and on the stove.

"I'm making you dinner. It's *my* way of apologizing." She shrugged.

"Ahh. Like minds."

"Seems so." She straightened and those gorgeous green eyes sparkled. "I've got dessert, too. We're eating in the dining room."

"Dining room? Is there a dress code?"

"Um, I bought a new dress—but you wear whatever you want."

She opened the fridge and withdrew a beer from the side door. Handing it to him, she said, "Why don't you go up and take a hot shower? Dinner will be ready in thirty minutes."

He nodded. "Sounds like a plan. Thanks." As Chase passed through the dining room, he saw the transformation. The room was usually just a table and chairs—he didn't need more since he ate his meals in the kitchen. He kept the dining room that the blueprints called for only because someday there might be a reason to use the room, or it would help with resale. Though he didn't see himself moving.

Megan had prettied up the room. She'd added a tablecloth, and there were candles on the table. He smiled.

Maybe I'm not as dead tired as I thought.

Not only was the dinner intended as an apology, but Megan also hoped to seduce Chase tonight. They'd been dancing around each other for weeks. For some noble reason that only Chase understood, he resisted everything but kissing. Every time things began to heat up, he'd cool them down.

She had a plan to move along with their relationship, and she was sticking to it.

Soon enough, they'd have to decide one way or another about their marriage. She expected a call from Rich any day with some big plan as to how they would spin the marriage and divorce. She wasn't ready. She wanted more time.

Dinner would set the mood, and hopefully, she was right that Chase needed only a nudge in the right direction. That he would recognize the gesture for what it was, and he would be on board to ramp up their relationship a notch or two.

She jogged up to her room to shower and style her hair for a change. Tying it up in a messy bun or ponytail was getting old. Besides, she was going for sexy, not practical tonight.

She took extra care with her makeup. She slipped on the emerald mini dress that complemented her hair and eyes. Nodding her approval in the mirror, she took a deep breath.

She knew how to play up her looks. The few years in the business taught her how to capture an audience's attention. And tonight, she was playing for an audience of one.

When she came back downstairs, Chase was lounging in his favorite chair. Brady was beside him, enjoying the scratches he was receiving.

Chase looked up and whistled.

You go, girl. She mentally high-fived herself.

"Wow. My own siren."

"What?"

"A siren. That's what I thought when I saw you sing that night in Vegas."

"Wait. We met at the bar after the show. It was a coincidence, right?" She watched his face for a clue. "Wasn't it a chance meeting?"

"Not exactly. I did see you perform earlier. But when we ran into one another later, you'd already had a few, and I guess it didn't seem important to mention."

She twisted her face. That didn't make sense. Did it?

Before she could think about it anymore, he said, "It was my lucky night."

"In more ways than one," she added.

He blushed. And it was endearing. It was rare that Chase got embarrassed.

She wanted to stick to her plan to seduce him. Any digging in their past didn't align itself to that end. Time to change the subject.

"Want to help me in the kitchen?"

"Sure. What can I do?"

"How about you pour us some wine while I get the casserole out of the oven?"

As they ate, they each shared bits and pieces of their lives. He talked about his life as a firefighter. "Why does your father object so much?"

"That's the million-dollar question." He shrugged. "I'm not sure he objects to me being a firefighter—he simply wants me to work at Devine Construction alongside him. If you figure it out, let me know."

"I know parent relationships aren't always simple or easy." She chuckled. "Take my mom and me. I couldn't wait to get away from here. I was lucky that Sonny Dawson took me under his wing. He looks out for his team. I'll always be grateful for the step up he gave me."

"Do you like touring?"

"I do, but life on the road isn't all that glamorous. The pace takes a toll on many people. Before the incident"—she waved her hand beside her neck— "the plan was to go out on tour with Sonny again. This time I was to be the opening act, not singing backup."

"Speaking of singing, you know that song you were bopping around the kitchen to this afternoon when I got home?" Chase asked.

"Uh-huh."

"The song reminded me..." He rubbed the back of his neck and cleared his throat. "That song has a lot of similarities to what happened to us. Art imitating life, I guess." His eyes narrowed, pinning her attention. "Megan, I need to ask. Are you embarrassed or ashamed of what happened between us in Las Vegas?"

She blinked. "What? No. First, it's not like I remember much of what did happen."

He raised a brow. "Okay, yes, I suppose the song is like what happened with us, but it's a song, that's all. I swear there's no hidden agenda.

"I love Carrie. I listen to her music all the time. It was pure coincidence that you came in on that particular song. If you'd come home two minutes earlier, I'd have been singing, 'Jesus, Take the Wheel.'" She shrugged, trying for a bit of levity.

"I'm only embarrassed that I don't remember our night together. More regret than embarrassment, I guess. But to everything else, no. It is what it is."

She turned the question on him. "How about you? Are you worried about your reputation if the town learns what happened?" She held her breath. His expression was unreadable.

"You don't have to feel guilty," she rushed into the silence. "You didn't do anything wrong. I like to think it was kismet that we ran into each other that night." Instead of replying, Chase looked down at his hands in his lap. Megan felt her patience run out. Damn it. This was not going in the direction she had planned. She couldn't even seduce a guy she knew was attracted to her. What was wrong with her?

Candlelit dinner, wine, and music. She needed a more direct approach because the boy sure wasn't picking up on any cues. She leaned forward, blowing out one candle, then the other. "Can I ask you something?"

He finally looked at her, raising his brow. "Sure."

"Do you remember what you said to me on your boat the night I came up to confront you about Vegas?

He nodded. Sitting up straighter, he scooted to the edge of the chair. At least she had his attention now.

"Did you mean what you said to me that night?"

He cocked his head. "You'll need to be more specific. We talked about several things that night, and a lot has happened since that weekend." His cagey answer made her smile.

She stood and moved, one slow step at a time, in his direction.

"You said that when we have sex again, it will be under ideal circumstances. You used the word *when*, not *if*."

When she was beside his chair, she caressed his jawline and leaned down, whispering in his ear, "I want to have sex, and this time, I promise I will remember it."

"Careful, Megan. I can only take so much temptation. I'm trying really hard to be a gentleman."

"How hard?"

He shifted in his seat.

"What if I don't want you to be a gentleman? My eyes are wide open. Are yours?"

In one fluid movement, she pulled the tie of the dress, causing it to slide down her body, pooling on the floor at her feet.

His eyes widened. "Shit, Megan," he whispered reverently. "They are now." He rubbed his hand across his smooth cheeks, down his neck, and tugged on the collar of his dress shirt.

Good start.

"It's time to put your money where your mouth is, Captain Devine."

Chase gulped, and words escaped him. Glad he hadn't swallowed his tongue, he scanned her body from her pink toenails to her smooth, tan legs. His gaze stalled at the skimpy pink panties.

He'd never seen a more beautiful woman.

Megan's sultry, raspy new voice teased his self- control and tested his patience. Chase alleviated some of the tightening in his groin by pushing back from the table and standing. As his gaze continued to travel up her body, his patience fell away along with her dress.

She wore a simple pink bra that matched her barely there panties. Her full, gorgeous breasts made his fingers tingle. He gave in to the temptation to touch her silky skin and ran the back of his hand over the curve of her breasts—a slow caress that made her shiver.

He could count the freckles on her bare shoulders, wanting to play connect the dots with his tongue.

Drawing her into his arms, he kissed her rosy lips. She opened her mouth, and his tongue tangled with hers. Pressed up against him, she could no doubt feel his obvious erection. His want. His need for her.

He pulled away from her mouth but kept her in the embrace. He tipped her chin up so he had a clear view of her face.

"Are you sure this is what you want?"

She nodded.

"I need to hear you say it."

"Yes. Yes, I'm sure. I want you, Chase."

Against his better judgment, he ignored his lingering guilt. He swung her into a fireman-carry over his shoulder, eliciting a gasp.

"Put me down." A gasp escaped as she slapped his back.

"Nope." He moved to the stairs with haste.

"Oh, so suave of you."

"You want suave or action?"

"Action, Captain Devine, definitely action." She laughed. "Oh my God, the last time you threw me over your shoulder was that time you and Kell caught me spying."

He froze mid-stride.

"Remember? You hauled me over your shoulder and tossed me in the lake."

His childhood was full of adventures and pranks with Kell. Megan usually tailed behind them, begging to be included. He broke his best friend's trust when he took advantage of the situation in Vegas. At least, that is how Kell would see it.

"Chase? What's wrong?"

He didn't answer, and she smacked his back harder. "Chase, talk to me. What's wrong?"

He set her down. "Look Megan, this is a bad idea."

She put her hands on her hips. "Are you serious? What just happened?" He looked around the room. Anywhere but at her. "Tell me."

Her eyes narrowed, and she crossed her arms over her chest. Does she realize that her stance accentuated her cleavage? He blinked the thought out of his mind.

"Oh, for the love of God, I thought we had moved past this."

"I'm trying to be a good guy here."

"Fine, but you're giving me whiplash."

"I'm sorry. You're Kell's little sister."

She sighed. "It doesn't feel like you're sorry. You have to let that go. And you sure as hell need to stop worrying about what happened in Las Vegas. It wasn't like you planned it. It happened. We were both there, and we fell into it. It was a long time ago. I'm a big girl. It doesn't matter what Kell thinks. Besides, what makes you so sure he wouldn't approve of his best friend and his sister getting together if it makes us happy?"

She tapped her foot as she waited for his response. Could he let the past go? He sure as hell wanted Megan.

He saw the uncertainty flash in her eyes, and he felt like a shit.

"Or is that even it? Maybe you don't want me as much as I want you. Am I misreading the signals?"

"God, no. Yes, I want you."

"Then why the hesitation? Because it's giving me a bit of a complex."

"No, it's not you. Never think that. It's me, I...."

Megan threw up her hands. "You know what? Forget it." She straightened her back. She would not beg this man for sex. She stepped away from him. He reached for her wrist, but she evaded him.

"Wait. You're right."

She glared at him. "Damn right I am. But don't do me any favors. And, by the way, my offer is no longer on the table. Good night." She stomped up the stairs and slammed the door to her bedroom.

Megan grabbed her robe from the end of the bed and tugged the sash around her middle. She turned on the bedside lamp and lay down. She would not cry. No way.

Emmie jumped up beside her, purring her greeting. "Hi, little fur ball. Come here and give me some love."

She'd be damned before she would make the first move again. The ball was in his court now. She couldn't figure him out. Most guys would jump at sex. And they'd both been thinking about it for days now. You could cut the sexual tension between them with a knife.

So, why had Chase decided to play the noble card?

Chapter 22

Megan wanted, needed to fill her day with more than cooking for the men at the fire station. She'd offered to lend a hand in the afternoons at Bea's. It would be only until Mrs. Small sold the business. In the meantime, it was the perfect temporary gig for someone whose stay in Lucky had an end date.

Megan enjoyed the easygoing atmosphere. Located on Main Street, in the center of town, it was a hubbub of activity and gossip. It gave her a chance to get reacquainted with the townspeople.

Perhaps they weren't as annoying as she once thought.

Megan had just finished stocking the cup sleeves and stoppers when her local doctor, Becca James came in, ordered her usual, and took a seat at one of the tables by the front window. "How was your appointment with Dr. Hartley?"

"He was cautiously optimistic, which I guess I have to take as good news. Thanks for the referral, by the way."

"Of course. You're welcome. Yes, I think it is good news. You've healed on the outside, but I'm concerned more with the internal bruises. How are you doing emotionally? Are you sleeping? What about those nightmares?"

Her nightmares had become less frequent since she'd been back in Lucky. Thanks, in part, to her nightly sleeping companions, Emmie and Brady. Emmie had always slept with her, then Brady deserted Chase to join the girls, though he moved back and forth from night to night. He was no dummy. He knew who filled his dog bowl.

She couldn't credit her restful nights to the badass fireman who slept in the next room. If anything, he'd caused her more sleepless nights lately.

However, the self-defense course at the community center was doing a lot to help her peace of mind. She had met other women who were survivors of violence. These brave women showed her there were always those less fortunate, someone who had a tougher situation to overcome.

It made her want to give something back, as a thank-you for helping her to get stronger and feel safer. She hadn't figured out what. But she would.

"The nightmares are pretty much gone. I'm feeling stronger. Though it has a lot to do with feeling safe here in Lucky." She smiled.

"Well, I have a very good friend from medical school. Dr. Sam Winston, he's a psychiatrist and works with people who have experienced violence. Anyway, if you would like to meet with him I'm happy to set it up."

"Thanks. I will keep that in mind. Hopefully, by the time I head back to Nashville, I'll be able to face anything that comes at me. I'd prefer it not be another stalker though." She rolled her eyes as a weak laugh escaped.

"Ahh, stalker humor." Becca chuckled. "So, at the risk of a very bad segue, how are things with Chase? I heard you're helping at the fire station. And staying at his place." Megan caught the sparkle in Becca's eyes.

"Fine, I guess. We've been friends for years."

"Uh-huh."

"Okay, as my doctor, there is the whole confidentiality thing, right?"

Becca cocked her head. "That only applies to health topics. How about a bond between two friends?"

"All right. So, oh my God, why does it have to be so complicated? The other night, I tried to seduce him, and it was a big fat failure."

"Oh?"

"Oh yeah. Big. Fat. Failure. I don't know what else to do. I know he cares about me. I know he finds me attractive. We've kissed several times. But it's like he can't get past the cursed friend thing. He's been a friend of our family for years. He's my big brother Kell's best friend."

And a dreamy kisser and great at sexy banter despite being the perfect gentleman and host. Damn it. Should she give seduction another chance? Could she face getting turned down yet again?

But it looked like if she wanted to have sex with Chase, she would have to be the one to push the agenda. They'd both qualify for the senior discount at Denny's out on Route 10 by the time she waited for him to make a move.

"I guess he feels like it's a betrayal to my brother." She shrugged.

"What does your brother think of the situation? Is he upset?"

"No. Well, he has no idea. He's a Marine over in the Middle East somewhere. This is his fourth tour."

"Mmm. I presume you've told Chase how you feel?"

"Um, sure. We have a bit of history. I won't go into it now. But there is a bond between us. But getting him to have sex with me has been unsuccessful." She shook her head. "Sheesh, you'd think it was torture for the poor guy."

"I've always believed honesty is the best policy. You need to lay it out there."

Stripping out of my dress and throwing myself at him... How much more out there can I get?

✦

It was a beautiful day, not a cloud in the sky, the sun reflecting off the blue lake. Usually, he'd be enjoying the quiet calm of floating on the lake. Drinking beer, fishing, and hanging with Brady always relaxed him.

But Chase's mood didn't match the day at all.

The beer tasted flat, the fish weren't biting, and even his faithful buddy seemed forlorn. The traitorous dog watched the shoreline as if they'd left someone behind. Shit, he couldn't see the logic of bringing a cat out on the boat. Cats and water didn't mix, right? Who'd have thought Brady and Emmie would have bonded so fast.

"Brady, come." He petted the dog's head and coaxed, "What's wrong, boy? Do you miss Emmie? I know how you feel. I miss Megan, too. I messed up. Didn't I?"

Brady seemed to nod. Of course, Brady would agree. He loved Megan.

"We were fine before the females came along, and we'll be fine when they leave. But today we're doing our guy thing. We don't need them to relax and have fun." He shook his head, chuckling. "I can't believe I'm having a one-sided conversation and trying to reason with my dog."

Or was he trying to convince himself?

He had more than his growing feelings for Megan and the other night's fiasco on his mind. Dad had left a message but didn't say what it was about. Dad never did, but Gerald Devine never missed an opportunity to pressure Chase to quit his job as a firefighter.

It was a different day, same argument.

Dad's latest attempt was more of the same, a combination of ranting, cajoling, and conniving. Chase couldn't understand why Mom never stepped in, but then again, he had never heard Mom contradict Dad on any matter. So why would she start now? Mom hadn't always been so aloof. But ever since Conner died, something inside her had died, too.

He wasn't sure which was harder to take, his father's loud demands or his mother's silence. Why couldn't his parents respect the career path he chose?

Chase sighed. Stowing his fishing gear, he turned the boat toward shore. Might as well face it head-on. He'd drive over to his parents' house on the other side of the lake to see about this latest issue.

If Dad could accept, and respect, Chase's decision, they could work out a compromise. He'd be willing to work part-time for the family's business. Or consult. He was confident if they gave it some thought, they could figure out a solution that made them both happy. But Dad was an all-or-nothing guy.

Twenty minutes before the end of her shift the bell above the door jingled.

"Be right with you," she called out.

"I'd hope so. Keeping a customer waiting is a bad business practice."

Megan recognized that voice. She spun around quickly, and the stack of cups she was stocking scattered all over the counter. "Kell," she squealed as she dashed across the room and jumped into his arms.

He hugged her tight. They held on to one another for several seconds. Neither spoke. Simply holding onto one another was enough. She'd missed him like crazy.

"Oh my God. Are you hurt? Does Mom know?" Her questions came in rapid succession. She'd hyperventilate from excitement if she weren't careful. She took a few big breaths. "What are you doing here?"

"Ordering a coffee and a muffin, what else?" Kell smirked.

"Yeah, okay. Whatever. Always the smart-ass." Megan playfully punched him in the arm.

He set her away from him so he could inspect her. His expression turned serious, and his eyes narrowed, no doubt because he saw the faint scar on her forehead. "I came as soon as I could. I had to wait for the paperwork to go through. I'm sorry." He studied her face as if he had never seen her before. "Are you really, all right? It sucked that I couldn't be here for you."

"I won't lie; it was scary." She shook the unhappy feelings aside. "But I'm doing better now. Especially since coming to Lucky."

He lifted a brow. "So, it was the right decision to come home?"

She laughed. "Yeah, yeah, you and Chase were correct. He made it clear that you thought it was for the best." She shrugged. "Since I'm so happy to see you, I won't give you a bunch of crap over it."

"That would be a first." He grinned.

She waved her hand. "Anyway, how long is your leave?"

He shook his head. "Not a leave. I'm done with my service. I got an honorable discharge. I don't know what I'm going to do now."

Megan gasped. "What? Are you okay?" In seconds, her happiness flipped to worry. She scanned his face then his body for evidence of an injury.

"I'm fine. It was past time for me to call it good."

Megan sighed, relieved. He was finally back home. In one piece. Then an uncomfortable thought came to her. "Did you do this because of me?"

He shook his head. "Don't flatter yourself."

She put her hands on her hips and glared.

"Okay, it was a little about you, but more about being time to get the hell out. Too much death and destruction. It takes a toll, you know?"

He was quiet for a moment. Then added, "My heart just wasn't in it anymore—not for a while, not since ..." He ducked his head. "Never mind. It doesn't matter."

She'd give him the time he needed, but eventually she'd get him to talk to her. She loved her big brother, and if there was something else going on, she wanted to be there for him.

He clapped his hands, shaking off the melancholy. "When you got attacked, I knew it was time to come home. At least if I was stateside, I could get to you if you needed me. I'm glad to see you're healing."

She nodded. "Thanks. I am." She squeezed his arm. "Oh my God. Wait until Mom hears you're home. She'll flip a switch."

He barked a laugh. "Ugh. Don't remind me. I'm afraid that's true."

She joined his laughter. "The Marines might look better after a few days with Mom. She has gotten bolder with age."

"Thanks for the heads-up."

"Sure." She'd fill Kell in on her prognosis later. It wasn't the best news, but it wasn't the worst either. "Does Chase know you're back?"

"Not yet. You're my first stop. I was driving past, on my way to the house, when I spotted"—he tugged on her ponytail— "this mass of curls through the front window. I did a U-turn right out in front of the square. I have to say, it was surprising to see you here, especially with an apron on."

"I know, right? I've been cooking breakfast for the men over at the fire station while their regular cook is on leave. And when I saw that Mrs. Small—you remember her—was having trouble finding help, I offered."

"Sure, I do. Johnny, Chase, and I used to come in here after baseball practice. Thought we were big deals. I'll never forget the first time we ordered an espresso. Johnny and I stomached it okay, but Chase, he turned green and ran to the bathroom to get sick." Kell laughed.

"I've never heard that story before."

"Because we didn't tell anyone. Not one of our smarter moments."

"I guess not. I haven't thought of Johnny in a long time. Do you stay in touch?"

"Off and on. Neither of us would win a prize for staying connected. He's still pitching. Life of a pro baseball player keeps him busy."

"Working here and at the fire station has been good for me. Too much idle time can lead to fear and anxiety about the attack. I'm working on it, though."

He nodded. "C'mere, sis." He hugged her. "I'm here now. Anything you need, don't hesitate."

"Thanks, Kell."

"I better leave you to it then. I'm headed to the fire station next, then I'll go home to see Mom."

"Oh, Chase is off today. He took his boat out to fish. Probably caught supper by now."

Kell arched a brow. "You know Chase's schedule?"

Oops. The cat didn't jump out of the bag—she'd dumped it out. Smooth. She bit her lip. Damn.

She thought about lying—because I work with him at the fire station. But Kell would find out sooner than later.

Chase was going to kill her for opening her big fat mouth. He'd want a chance to talk to Kell about their living arrangements. Not that there was anything to tell. Nope, it was freaking platonic, despite her effort to change it. Not a big deal. She needed to relax. Play it cool.

"So, here's the thing," she said.

"Yes, I'm listening," Kell said, chuckling.

She took a deep breath. "I've been staying at Chase's place."

His eyes narrowed. "Why?"

"I was having trouble sleeping at mom's house, and I needed to rest to recuperate, so Chase stepped up and saved the day. Simple as that. Strictly platonic. Plus, I have my cat. Remember, Mom can't be around cats."

She hid her crossed fingers behind her back.

Chase docked his boat, killing the engine as an incoming text beeped. He almost ignored it, thinking it would be from Dad. But perhaps there was an emergency at the fire station. His pulse sped up when he saw Megan's name.

Megan: *Guess what? Kell's home. Yea. He's heading over. (Happy face emoji)*

Kell was home. Several emotions bombarded him at once: Surprise. Joy. Guilt. Worry. He called Brady to jump off the boat, then he looked up to see Kell striding down the gradual sloped lawn to the dock. The man looked like he was on a mission. It was definitely his warrior's face.

Shit. Had Megan told Kell about Vegas? That would suck, but at least it would finally be out in the open.

Chase would protect Megan no matter what, so he was determined to take whatever shit Kell was about to give him. Vegas was all on him. He sighed and braced himself.

Kell swung his arm out and grabbed Chase in a bear hug. "I missed you, bro," Kell said.

Chase shook his head to dislodge his confusion and hugged his friend back. "Kell, it's great to see you. When did you get back?"

"In the States, about forty-eight hours ago. In Lucky, about an hour ago."

Brady wagged his tail like crazy and waited impatiently for his turn to be greeted. Kell didn't disappoint. He knelt and scratched Brady's back.

"Hey, Brady. Good to see you again. You sure are a happy dude, aren't you?"

Brady barked.

"Come on up to the house."

The two men strode up the path, with Brady leading the charge.

"Beer?" Chase offered.

"Sounds good. Didn't catch anything?" Kell inclined his head toward the lake.

Chase frowned. "Nope, bad day for fishing. In fact, before you arrived, I was commiserating with Brady here on what a shitty day it was. But your arrival has changed that."

He handed Kell a bottle.

"Thanks."

Chase clinked his beer bottle against his friend's.

"Welcome home, buddy."

Chapter 23

Megan got home around seven. *Wait, this isn't your home.* She was a guest in Chase's home. He wasn't interested in moving their friendship to the next level. He'd made that clear enough.

On the other hand, he was her legal husband. Maybe she needed to approach this situation from that angle.

One thing was certain. She couldn't take any more of his mixed signals. Heated kisses one moment, then pushing her away the next. She wouldn't be embarrassing herself again.

There was no sign of Kell, so she assumed he'd left for home. She heard the shower running in Chase's bathroom. She needed a shower, too. Her hair reeked of coffee after her shift at Bea's.

Megan headed straight up to the hall bathroom. As she turned on the faucet, she smiled to herself, hoping Chase had gotten a blast of cold water. Served him right.

Captain Devine, Superhero of Ambivalence.

Afterward, she felt like a new woman. If not new, at least better than before. The scent of coffee on her skin and in her hair washed away along with her exhaustion from her long day.

She looked around the bathroom and realized she hadn't grabbed a change of fresh clothes. Damn. And she had planned to do a load of towels but hadn't. Double damn.

Now she only had a tiny, very inadequate towel.

She could get to her room before Chase finished dressing if she hurried.She listened for any telltale signs that Chase was done with his own shower, but she heard nothing.

She'd have to chance it. If she hurried, she could get to her room before Chase finished dressing. She secured the towel as best she could and darted out of the bathroom.

Whoomph.

She yelped as Chase slammed into her. Her death grip on the towel turned her knuckles white.

Of course, Chase was jogging past at the exact same moment she tried to get across the hall.

"Sorry," he said, reaching out to steady her. He, too, had on only a towel. She took a step back, afraid his towel would slip right off his slim hips.

Could their timing get any worse?

"I left my clean laundry downstairs. I was making a run for it, figuring you'd be in there for a while." He shrugged. "My timing sucks."

"Seems to be the story of our lives." She took a step to pass him, but he put a hand on her arm.

"About the other night—"

She shook her head. "No, let's not revisit that embarrassing scene."

"Megan..."

"Don't worry. I won't throw myself at you again. I'm sorry I put you in an awkward position, especially when you have been so generous in letting me stay here."

"That's just it. I was wrong. I keep making the same mistake. But I can't stop thinking about you.

I swear I can still smell your perfume hours after you've left the firehouse. I'm tired of fighting this."

"Gee, thanks. Not exactly what a girl wants to hear. Look, don't do me any favors. You don't have to worry about Kell finding out. As far as he knows, we're nothing more than old friends and roommates."

"That isn't what I meant. All I ever wanted was to look out for you. Protect you. My guilt over Vegas wasn't just about Kell or thinking it was a mistake. It's that you deserved better than a one-night stand."

He still hung onto her arm. She was about to shake loose when he pulled her up against his still-damp, warm chest. Her fingers itched to explore his soft brown chest hair. None of that manscaping crap. She preferred a man who looked like a man.

Her gaze drifted lower to where the hair narrowed, leading below his towel, and the evidence of an impressive bulge. Her grip loosened on her own towel, causing it to reveal a breast.

He released his hold on her arm and touched the exposed nipple.

She ached to run her hands along his firm abs and impressive biceps. She craved his touch. Oh, what the hell. She buried her face in the crook of his neck, the scent of a freshly showered male irresistible. Her pheromones hit a high C.

Chase tilted her head and slipped his tongue between the seam of her lips.

Would he stay the course this time or back off?

Brady appeared out of nowhere, tangling between the two of them. He must have realized there was activity happening in the house without him.

Chase pulled away from her and used his dog-daddy voice. "Sorry, buddy. This is a party for two. No pets allowed. Be a good dog and go back downstairs to your bed." He pointed in the directions of the stairs.

"Aww, poor Brady. Did you see that pathetic, sad face? How could you?" She giggled.

Chase didn't answer. He simply backed her up, right into his bedroom, and shut the door. She said nothing. She didn't want to break the spell with talk. In fact, she held her breath, hoping he wouldn't change his mind again.

He laid her down on his bed. Skin on skin. This was what she'd wanted for so long. To feel him as he pressed his body down on hers.

The towels were no longer covering anything and were more of a hindrance, so she yanked hers off, and he did the same. He was hard and ready for her. He kissed his way from her neck down to her breasts, taking his time exploring them.

Finally, he said, "I want to make this good for you. Special. But I gotta tell you, I've kept this need bottled up inside me for so long. I'm not sure how long I can last."

"That's all right. This first time I'll give you a pass." She grinned. "The second time, you'll need to work a little harder to rock my world."

"Yes, ma'am, that I can do." He suited up and when he finally pushed into her, she was wet and ready. "You're really tight."

Breathless, she replied, "Uh-huh. Don't stop."

"You're so tight."

"Um, you just said that."

"Did I? Guess I'm delusional. But you are."

"Well, it *has* been two years."

He froze and looked down into her face. For a second, she feared she'd said too much again. Would he pull away?

"There's been no one else since..."

She shook her head. "I've been too busy with my career. There's been no one else." Despite her actions in Las Vegas, she was a small-town girl at heart. Gratuitous sex was not her thing. Besides, she'd never gotten past her crush on Chase.

He smiled as he leaned down and took her mouth. Kissing her, he thrust into her again. His kiss grew in intensity as the momentum built and their bodies connected intimately. Her moans matched his. Finally, she cried out when her orgasm came, and he came just seconds later. He held her tight as their breathing calmed.

This was what she'd been wanting for so long.

"Chase," she whispered, "um, how was that compared to our night in Las Vegas?"

He kissed her forehead. "Even better. It was incred—ow." he howled.

She gasped.

In one fluid motion, Emmie had pounced on Chase's back. He rolled away from Megan, flipping the cat off his back. The cat landed on her feet beside the bed and gave a loud, indignant meow.

"Damn cat."

"Oh, my poor baby. Come here, baby girl." Megan looked at Chase and giggled.

"What is she doing in here?"

"I don't know why she's in your bedroom. She must have been sleeping under the bed. I'm sorry." More giggling. "I shouldn't laugh, but your face was priceless. I can't believe my little kitty scared you, the big, heroic firefighter."

He frowned. "She didn't scare me. She startled me. And scratched my back. Did she draw blood?"

"Let me see." He turned so she could see his back.

"Nope, just a teeny-tiny scratch. Want me to kiss it and make it all better?"

Nodding, he relaxed back on the bed. "Yeah, that sounds like a good plan."

"Then finish rolling over."

"Yes, ma'am." He might be the one to give the orders at the fire station, but he seemed more than willing to take orders from her.

"From now on, I'm keeping my bedroom door closed. No more sneak attacks."

❧

After their busy and thorough night of sexual calisthenics, Megan left Chase's bed while he still slept. Thinking about last night left her fanning the warmth that crept from her neck to her face.

But right now, she had a hot breakfast to prepare for the firefighters.

She'd started the coffee and was just scrambling the eggs when her cell phone rang.

"Hello, dear brother. This is awfully early, even for you."

"Okay, smart-ass, you're hilarious," Kell said.

"Good morning to you, too." Hopefully, her saccharine tone carried over the line. "Get a good night's sleep?"

"You know damn well I didn't."

"Oh really? Why's that?"

"You set me up. You knew Mom and what's his name would go at it like fucking rabbits."

"Hmm. Great description. Accurate, too." She snickered.

"Are you laughing? Do you know how difficult it is to get to sleep when your mother is having loud sex down the hall? Shit, I bet she keeps the neighbors up."

"Try being in the room next door."

"Of course, you know. That's why you moved out to Chase's place."

She laughed full out now, letting him hear her amusement. "I thought you needed to get indoctrinated back into life at the Howard house."

"I owe you. Remember, payback can be a bitch." Finally, he let out a laugh. "Wham, wham, wham, all night long."

She wiped the tears of amusement from her eyes. "Listen, I've got to start breakfast. Chase is still off today—why don't you go out to his place for a visit? Go out on his boat. Do a little fishing. You can always catch a nap if the fish aren't biting. It's tranquil out on the lake."

Megan heard indistinct grumbling but ignored it. "I'll see you later. Hey, tell Chase I'll check with him later to see if he catches anything. If not, I'll pick up takeout for supper. We can eat on the patio. It's supposed to be a nice evening."

The supper cleanup had been quick and easy. Subs were an easy fix. Not fancy, but filling. She'd bought macaroni salad, chips, and grapes to round out the meal and stopped at Bea's to get the double fudge brownies for dessert. What a perfect picnic supper with the two most important men in her life.

The mood was mellow. Brady snoozed, sprawled out next to Chase's chair. He'd worn himself out from the nonstop game of catch he'd coaxed Kell into playing.

Emmie didn't like it, but she was an indoor cat. She stood at the slider, watching—or lurking, according to Chase. He now considered her a dangerous feline.

Megan filled them in on her most recent appointment at the Cleveland Clinic. She hadn't discussed the doctor visit and the recommended rehab plan in much detail before.

A kernel of an idea had rooted itself in her brain, and she couldn't shake it. It was time to get some input.

She'd been back in Lucky for over six weeks, and already she was feeling like this was home. What was different now? Was Chase the reason? At any rate, she was giving thoughts to putting down some roots in Lucky.

"I've had an idea mulling around in my head for a week."

Chase and Kell looked at each other and both said, "Uh-oh," at the same time.

"Ha ha, you're so *not* funny. Just listen to this idea with an open mind. I'm thinking about buying Bea's place."

Both men stared at her with baffled expressions.

"Bea hasn't had a nibble on the place. She's ready to move to Florida to be with her sisters. She's not getting any younger. Her words, not mine. Let's face it. It's Lucky. There isn't a boon of buyers. I have plenty of money saved up. If I pay what she's asking, it will give her a nice tidy sum to start her retirement."

Megan waited for their responses. They'd be skilled poker players because neither had a tell.

Finally, Kell said, "I don't know. The obvious question is, why would you want to buy a local business when you live in Nashville?"

Chase scooted to the edge of his seat.

"For one thing, we don't know how long my rehab will take. It's not like I can start singing again right away, even if I were to head home."

Could she go back to Nashville while Jason was still at large? The cops were keeping her informed, but there'd been nothing yet. His trail had gone cold.

As if he could read her mind, Chase said, "Your external bruises are barely visible, and the cuts have healed nicely. But I worry about your emotional state. The stalker played mind games with you, and the asshole is still out there."

Megan took several deep breaths to keep from getting light-headed. Then she kept her breathing even. She wouldn't allow thoughts of Sykes to scare her. She was stronger than that.

"Is that part of it, Megan?" Kell asked, his big brother concern clear. "Are you uncomfortable with the idea of going back to Nashville?"

She clasped her hands between her legs to hide her nervousness. "The idea of him still being out there doesn't sit well with me. I'm definitely more relaxed here in Lucky. I'm not sure how safe I'll feel when I get back to Nashville."

She shrugged. "But I want to help Bea. The idea of owning a business intrigues me."

Straightening her posture, she continued, "I have lots of ideas on how to grow the business. There's that empty building next door. I could buy that place, too, and then knock out the wall and—"

"Whoa, whoa, whoa," Chase interjected. Brady lifted his head at the louder tone, saw that Chase was fine, then plopped his head back down. "You're thinking of buying two buildings? Expanding? That's a big plan."

"I know. I've sketched a few drawings to show you."

Scooting back from the table, Kell said, "This is out of my area of expertise. If you need my help with an insurgence of some kind, I'm your man. Although, come to think of it, I can wield a mean hammer.

"However, is this what you really want? What happens when you go back to Nashville? Because this guy is going to get caught and you will get your voice back." His stare penetrated her comfort level.

Megan hated when he pulled the *I'm older and wiser* card.

She brushed aside his question like a lackluster welcome at the Grand Ole Opry. With the same determination that she had shown before, when no one believed in her dream to become a singer, she was certain she could do it again. "I'm not worried about that. I just want—no, I need a project. Something to focus on. Cooking at the station is fine. I love it."

She got on a roll, and her excitement bubbled out of her. "But that hardly fills my day. And Char will be back soon, and then I won't be needed. This is something I can do for the community."

The two men in her life nodded with little enthusiasm.

She refused to let them discourage her. What did they know?

"Hold up, sis—let's look at this another way. Do you think Lucky can sustain another business?"

"It won't be another business." She shook her head. "The plan would be to buy an established business with a loyal customer base."

Kell frowned. "Don't you need a business plan? You'll need more to go on than that."

She frowned.

Looking at Chase, he said, "You're unusually quiet. You've lived and worked in Lucky, while Megan and I took off. Your family has a construction business." Kell arched a brow. "What are your thoughts?"

Chase cleared his throat. "The building in question, the old drugstore, on the north side of the Beanery, has been sitting empty for several years now. It'll take a lot of work to bring it up to code."

Her frown deepened. "How much is a lot?"

"I don't know. But the place is in rough shape. New electrical and plumbing for a start."

She narrowed her eyes and glared at Chase. Why was he being such a Debbie Downer? Or, rather, a David Downer. Was this his way of giving her a reality check? Well, no thanks. "So, I'll make an appointment with your father this week, see if he can do a walk-through with me and give me an estimate."

"You need to slow down," said Chase.

She stood, shoving her hands on her hips. "Don't tell me what I should or shouldn't do. I can and will make my own decisions. I don't need you to give me permission."

Frowning, Chase shook his head and stood up to face off with her.

"You haven't considered what will happen when you go back to Nashville. Because last I knew, you were only here to recover and then you'll be back to your singing career. What will you do with a business here?"

"I can hire a staff. Owning a business in Lucky doesn't mean I can't continue my music career. The two are not mutually exclusive."

Her brother watched the two of them bicker. Crap. She'd forgotten Kell's ability to assess a situation quickly and accurately. His hawk-eyed awareness had kept him alive all these years.

Sure enough, Kell scooted forward on his chair and set his beer on the table. "Okay, who wants to tell me what's going on between the two of you?"

"Nothing," both Megan and Chase said simultaneously.

Damn, that doesn't sound suspicious at all.

Chase studied Megan's face, trying to get a read.

How could they keep their relationship from Kell? He was his best friend. Besides, Kell deserved to know the truth. At least the *recent* truth. But Chase didn't want to say anything without talking to Megan first.

Their relationship was at a fragile stage. A new beginning. Hopefully, at least their second act was new.

As if they didn't already have a balancing act, now she was proposing a large project. She didn't know what she was in for, but it would be a challenge to get through to this tenacious woman.

First things first.

He cleared his throat. "Megan, can you give me a hand in the kitchen?"

She nodded but continued to glare at him, grumbling, "Sure." Patting Kell's knee, she added, "Be right back. Want another beer or anything?"

Kell shook his head. "No, I'm good." His intense gaze followed them off the patio and into the house. Chase closed the swinging door for the privacy and pulled her to the farthest corner of the kitchen. But before he could say anything, she muttered, "Why are you being Captain Doom and Gloom?"

They could fight about that later.

"We should come clean with Kell." Chase got right to the point.

"I think... wait, what?"

"You heard me."

"So, we aren't discussing you raining on my happy parade?"

He shook his head. "Not now. First, we're going to talk about our relationship. I'm tired of pretending there's nothing between us. We both know that isn't true. We danced around our mutual attraction for weeks. And finally, we got past the dance, and now I don't want to keep my hands to myself. I want to kiss you. Touch you. I'm done hiding. We need to tell him. We need to tell everyone."

She shook her head. "We can't. Not yet anyway. I haven't heard from Rich."

"Your manager is deciding about your personal life now?"

"No, of course not. But he makes decisions that affect my career." Her voice grew louder than a whisper. "And you know how my mom is and this gossip-fueled town."

"Your brother isn't stupid. He knows something's up between us."

Megan put her hands on her hips. "He can speculate all he wants. This is my life, and I don't need my big brother or anyone else sticking their nose into it. Are you worried he might kick your ass?"

"I wasn't. But thanks for bringing it up."

She smirked.

He didn't think Kell would have a problem with them being in a relationship now. What Chase feared was Kell learning the truth of what happened in Vegas. That would deserve an ass-kicking.

"Kell will need a place to crash—I won't turn him away. Where does that leave us? I don't want to be sneaking around behind his back," Chase said.

She sighed. "Me neither. Okay, you're right. But he must promise not to tell Mom." She shook her finger. "You know how she is. Your folks, too."

"We're only postponing the inevitable. People will figure it out. Some guys at the fire station have been asking me questions about us."

"What are they asking?"

He shook his head. "It doesn't matter. I've put them off for now. But do you know how hard it is to keep my hands off you?"

He kissed her, pushing her up against the counter, pressing their bodies together. They were catching their breaths when the door swung open and Kell strolled in. He stopped just inside the room, legs apart with his hands on his hips, looking every bit a Marine.

He cleared his throat for just for the effect because it wasn't like they wouldn't notice him. "For a builder, you should know how to soundproof better."

Chapter 24

Megan's face turned a beautiful shade of pink. "Kell," she croaked.

Chase set her aside, facing Kell. "Megan has always had a difficult time keeping her volume on low."

"And you were outside on the patio," she added.

"So, you two have something you want to tell me?"

"We're sleeping together," Megan blurted.

Chase cringed at her bluntness. Got to hand it to her. She wasn't afraid to jump right in.

"And I don't want to hear any lectures from my big brother. And don't frown at Chase."

Chase raised his eyebrows, interjecting, "It's more than *sleeping together.*" Why did he sound defensive?

"Why would I object? It's not like you're a naïve girl. Because in that case, I would have to kick his ass," Kell said.

Chase swallowed. Hopefully, Megan would keep quiet about their past—for now. It was only a matter of time before he'd have to own up to what happened in Las Vegas and why he was there. But for now, it was nice for his best friend to be supportive.

Kell needed to see that Chase and Megan were good together. Because if he had any hope at all of convincing Megan that they belonged together, it couldn't hurt to have Kell's support.

🍀

Megan couldn't tell if Chase worried by Kell's *kick his ass* comment?

If he was a bit piqued, she couldn't tell because he excused himself to take Brady on his evening walk around the lake.

Did Chase want them to keep quiet about how they'd hooked up in Las Vegas? It was a delicate situation. Until they heard from Rich, it was best to keep that information between the two of them.

She glared at Kell. "There'll be no ass kicking."

She couldn't read her brother's face. "You ready for another beer now?"

"Sure."

She grabbed a beer and poured another glass of wine for herself, then moved into the living room.

"Is this new between you two?" Kell did not try to hide his smirk.

"Yes, and no. We've texted and chatted over the years, but it wasn't until he came down to Nashville and brought me back here that the sparks ignited." She grinned at her brother. Taunted him. Dared him to give her the third degree as if she were a teenager.

He nodded. "I was planning to ask Chase if I could crash here rather than at home. That is out of the question now."

She raised a brow. "Why?"

He cringed. "Because I don't want a repeat of the wall-banging I experienced at home." A mock shiver emphasized his point.

She rolled her eyes. "Chase and I have a little more self-control than that. But suit yourself." She shrugged. "Where will you stay instead?"

He opened his mouth to answer, but she cut in before a word came out. "No, wait, I have the perfect place. It's small but clean."

Kell leaned forward, his elbows on his knees, his curiosity piqued. "I'm listening."

"There's a studio apartment above Bea's place. Her last tenant moved out a few months ago, and since she planned to sell the place, she didn't bother to rent it again. I'm confident that you can reach a compromise. And just think, if I buy the place, I'll be your landlord."

Grinning, she rubbed her hands together with fiendish glee.

Kell's loud laugh caught Chase's attention when he came back in the room with a cheerful Brady. He tossed the tennis ball, asking, "What's so funny?"

"Megan was telling me about the apartment above Bea's. She told me she'd be my landlord if she bought the business.

Chase joined Kell in a laugh.

Frowning, Megan said, "I don't see what's so funny."

"You don't know the first thing about being a landlord or how to fix anything," Chase said.

She huffed. "I can learn."

Both men nodded, but their grins told another story.

"Whatever. It's time for me to go to bed. I have an early morning at the fire station." She stood. "I'll leave you two to snicker by yourselves. Good night."

She stomped toward the stairs, then paused and turned around. "Kell, can you keep quiet about Chase and me? We have been keeping it private. I certainly don't want Mom to know. At least not yet."

"Sure." He drew his finger across the seam of his lips. "My lips are sealed."

"Thanks. Now, if you two will excuse me, I'm going upstairs. Night."

"Night," they replied in unison.

The following Monday, after she left the fire station, Megan drove to Devine Construction on the outskirts of town. Chase's family business had an excellent reputation for quality design and attention to fine details.

A young woman looked up from her typing. "Good afternoon. May I help you?"

"I'm Megan Howard." A big smile formed on the young woman's face. "I know who you are. I'm a big fan. The whole town is proud of you."

"Thank you." Megan's face flushed. She still wasn't completely comfortable being recognized or the adoration from fans.

"Your mom keeps us updated on your news. Of course, when 'Honkytonk Angel' came out, we all knew you were making it down there in Nashville," she gushed.

Megan nodded. "That's very nice. I was hoping to see Mr. Devine if he's in. Or someone who could discuss a possible renovation project with me."

The receptionist glanced at the phone on her desk. "Mr. Devine's extension is lit up, but I'll let him know you're here."

While she waited, Megan scanned her phone for messages and emails. A few minutes later, Mr. Devine walked in. "Megan Howard. I heard you were back in town. Look at you. All grown up."

Gotta love that Lucky grapevine.

She returned a halfhearted smile. She knew all about the tug-of-war he had going with Chase.

"Nice to see you again, Mr. Devine. How are you?"

"Fine, fine. I'll be even better when I can finally retire, move south. Enjoy a daily game of golf with my friends."

Chase had confided to her that his father was using his *need to retire* as a maneuvering tactic to get Chase on board.

Still, she grew uncomfortable as the man studied her. She shifted from foot to foot. Finally, he narrowed his eyes. "Aren't you staying at my son's place?"

She narrowed her eyes right back at him. "Yes, I am." There was no way she would discuss anything personal with this man. "My mother is deathly allergic to cats, and since I brought my cat along, Chase graciously offered me his guest room." So what if there was a little more to the story than that? She would share nothing else.

"Hmm, perhaps you can help me persuade that stubborn son of mine to come to work with me."

"Mr. Devine, I wouldn't dream of interfering in Chase's life like that. Especially since I know how much he loves what he does."

He frowned, then gave her a curt nod. "What can I help you with today?"

She took a deep breath and got straight to the point. "I'm considering buying the vacant building next to Bea's. I'd like someone to walk through it with me to get an idea of how much renovation it'll need. And how expensive it would be to make the changes I want. That way, I can make a more informed decision."

After a moment, Gerald said, "All right, I'll arrange for one of my supervisors to meet you there. Let's check with Janie—she knows where we are at any time of the day."

"Thank you," Megan replied.

"What the hell?" Chase muttered to himself as he passed through downtown on his way to the hardware store. Ted Reed, one of Dad's supervisors, was entering the vacant building next to Bea's, with a familiar redhead leading the way.

She must have gone through with her idea to get his dad's help. He didn't think she'd do it this fast. That woman was stubborn and a reckoning force. Her working with his dad would have been bad enough but Ted the Tool. Nope. No way.

He made a U-turn in the middle of Main Street and parked next to the Devine Construction truck. Ted earned his nickname back in high school. How ironic that he ended up in the construction business.

Chase doubted Megan would be the exception. Ted was bound to turn on his charm. Could he blame the guy, though? As far as the town knew, Megan and Chase were merely friends. Nothing more.

Relieved to find the door unlocked, he entered and followed the sound of Megan's sexy rasp. Her light laughter stopped him in his tracks. He'd bet that son of a bitch was flirting with her.

It was time for them to come clean. He wanted to show Reed that Megan was not available.

Stomping into the back room, he paused in the doorway just in time to see Ted lean into Megan's personal space. She immediately took a step away. Had Chase not been watching her face, he might have missed the flash of wariness in her eyes. He recognized her body language loud and clear.

Of course, she would have residual fears when in a dark, vacant building with a strange man. His jealousy morphed into protectiveness. Damn his dad for pawning her off on someone else rather than doing it himself.

"Megan. Sorry I'm late. I missed your message about this meeting."

"Chase," she exclaimed. Was that relief he saw on her face?

Ted the Tool whipped his head around, narrowing his eyes. "Hey, Devine. What brings you by this afternoon?"

Chase walked straight to Megan, ready to pull her into his arms and kiss her to send Reed a message. Megan belonged to him. He stopped short. He couldn't kiss her. Not if they were keeping their relationship on the down low. Which was what they agreed, except for Kell.

"Chase, what are you doing here?" Megan asked.

He figured he'd get an earful later. But he wasn't going to leave Reed alone with his girl.

He directed his words to Reed. "I want to be here for Megan. This will be a big undertaking, and I want to help if I can. Lend moral support if she needs it. The building is due for an inspection, so I figured I could get a head start on that."

Liar.

He told the voice in his head to shut up.

Besides, he was only half lying. They needed to inspect the building before any construction could take place. But he already knew the condition of the property from the previous inspections. It could only be worse.

Megan would not be happy to hear that the building wasn't structurally sound. The electrical wiring would need to be completely redone. Plumbing too. It'd need a new heating and cooling system. Not cheap, and that was before they even got to the cosmetic changes she'd want to make.

They walked from room to room, with Megan explaining what she envisioned for the space. Knocking down a wall here, adding a wall there.

When they moved to the stairs, he called out, "Hold up. We need to grab a couple of flashlights. That is a steep stairwell, and it's been a while since anyone has been in here."

Once they were upstairs, it wouldn't be so bad since there were windows letting in the light.

"Ted, you grab yours—I'll get mine." Flashlights were a standard item they kept in all the company trucks. "Megan, we'll be right back," Chase said as he jogged to the front door.

He beat Ted back inside and wasn't surprised to have Megan giving him her very best stink-eye. "What are you doing here? You and Kell were quite clear on your thoughts about this building." She put her hands on her hips. "And it looked like you were about to get territorial and out us." She punched him in the arm. "What gives?"

"Nothing. I thought you could use another pair of eyes. I saw you coming in on my way to the hardware store. Why wouldn't I want to help you out?"

"Hmm, I don't know. Maybe because you and Kell seemed to think it is a lame-brained idea."

"No, we don't."

He held up the big flashlight. "Okay. Got my light. Let's check out the upstairs," Ted called out.

The guy was all business now.

But for good measure Chase held up his even bigger flashlight.

She didn't know what Chase was up to exactly. She half expected him to compare whose flashlight was bigger.

She should be angry at him for nearly outing their relationship with his Neanderthal behavior. Though she had to admit, she was relieved to see Chase. Ted Reed had been making her uncomfortable with his aggressive come-ons.

A cautionary flutter of panic had awakened in her belly as she'd walked into the dark, empty building with the man. Damn it. When would she be able to live her life without fear? She had to overcome this—and she would.

Her sensible, non-threatened side acknowledged that Ted was probably a good guy.

But she only had eyes for her sexy firefighter.

As it turned out, she enjoyed having Chase along for the walk-through. Wasn't that what she had envisioned in the first place? Work alongside one another to turn Bea's into something new for Lucky? Sure, she could do it on her own, but doing it with Chase would be so much better.

So regardless of his reason for being there, she went along with it.

The second floor was a big open room filled with clutter. It would take some work to clear it out. But this area was perfect for what she wanted it used for. She envisioned art classes. Or those paint-by-wine nights she and her girlfriends enjoyed in Nashville.

Megan could open the space for book clubs, knitting circles, quilters, and even support groups. She was most eager about the latter possibility. She would invite counselors to use the facility for group sessions for victims of violence. Her own experience told her there was a need.

Her nightmares had subsided once she felt safe again. Both her mind and body were healing, and a lot of that had to do with Chase. His home felt safe.

Chase cleared his throat. "Megan."

"What? Sorry."

"Ted asked whether you wanted to update the plumbing on this floor."

Ted had a huge tape measure in his hand, measuring the east wall where there was an itty-bitty bathroom. He turned to her and said, "We can upgrade and get the bathroom in working order. It depends on what you plan to do with the space. We could knock the east wall out of here to gain you another five to six square feet."

"You'll need to keep in mind fire codes," Chase said.

Ted nodded. "Goes without saying."

"Hmm. I'll need to think about that. Could you write up the quote with both options? Having a nice bathroom up here would be handier than having people running up and down the stairs. When I see the numbers, I'll decide."

"Sounds good." Ted closed his notepad and clicked off his pen.

"Ted, I'm heading your way." Ted gave him a quizzical stare, and Chase said, "Need to talk to my dad. See you later at home, Megan." He waggled his eyebrows and gave her a quick wink.

Laughing, she whispered for his ears only, "Promises, promises."

Chapter 25

Chase anticipated a battle with Megan over the fire and building codes. There was a lot she'd have to deal with before she could move forward with her renovation.

He hated being the one to thwart her enthusiasm, but all these complications could extend the timeline. What had she called him? Captain Doom and Gloom? He suppressed a small chuckle. She had to know he was happy for her. He tried to be as encouraging as he could, but facts were facts. The upgrades had to be done.

She was excited about all the possibilities they'd discussed. He just didn't want her to get so frustrated that she gave up.

He hadn't allowed himself to dream of her staying in Lucky, starting a life here with him. Whenever hope began to creep into his thinking, he'd ask himself, "What do I have to offer her?" He sure as shit couldn't compete with her glamorous life. If that was what she still craved, he might as well admit defeat.

All he could do was move forward. He'd help her if he could. He loved her. Even if she easily drove him nuts over one thing or another.

After the walk-through, he skipped the hardware store and drove out to Devine Construction.

Dad's truck was parked in his usual spot. No one was at the front desk, so Chase went straight to Dad's office, gave a quick tap, and marched in, hands on his hips.

Dad looked up with a frown at the interruption, a pen poised in his right hand. "What can I do for you?"

No reason not to get right to it. "Why did you send Ted Reed to do the walk-through with Megan?"

Dad lifted a brow. Setting the pen down, he studied Chase. He took his time rolling his chair back from the desk and stood. "Why wouldn't I send one of my top men? What's it to you, anyway? You've made it very clear that you want nothing to do with the company." He walked around his desk, folding his arms at his waist.

"You should've gone yourself. She's still jumpy after the attack."

Dad narrowed his eyes. "Are you telling me that Reed did something inappropriate?"

Chase jammed his hands into his pockets. "No. That isn't what I'm saying. But Megan is still apprehensive around strange men."

Dad relaxed. "Good. He talks a big game, but I don't think he'd push himself on a woman."

"No, but I wish you'd been more sensitive."

Dad looked chagrined. "How did you know I sent Reed?"

"I was driving by and saw him get out of the company truck. I made a U-turn on Main and joined the party."

"If you're that worried, I'd be more than happy to put you in charge of the renovation."

Now he saw the truth. Why hadn't he figured it out sooner?

Because he still hoped that Dad wasn't the cold, conniving bastard, he proved himself to be too many times to count.

"This was all about getting me to work here." He ran his hand through his hair. "You're un-fucking believable."

"Watch your mouth and tone with me."

"Why? What are you gonna do? Cut me off? I'm thirty-two years old." He stomped to the open office door. "I'm not playing your manipulation game."

His father remained where he stood with his arms crossed.

"If I help Megan, it will be my decision and on my time. It will have nothing to do with Devine Construction."

Disgusted, he shook his head. "Why aren't you willing to compromise and let me set my own terms? Why does everything have to be your way? If Conner were alive, you'd have your son to take over the business. I'm sorry he's gone, but I'll be damned if you'll control my life." Chase didn't wait for a reply.

A minute later, he slammed the door of his truck and pounded the steering wheel, hoping to vent some of the anger before he had to be back at the fire station. It was always the same. Round and round they went.

Damn that man.

Was that a flicker of pain he saw in Dad's eyes when he mentioned Conner's name? Why couldn't Dad and Mom see that the reason he was a firefighter was to save another family from losing a loved one? Chase shouldn't still care, but he did. Dad acted like Chase, wanting to be a firefighter was a direct insult to him.

Nothing he said or did could persuade them to be happy that he'd found a career he loved. It didn't matter to them that Chase was following his own dream.

Sighing, he put the truck in gear. He'd make a quick stop at the hardware store, then head back to the fire station.

"Well, young lady, I'm very pleased with the further healing to your throat and vocal cords. You've noticed a difference, haven't you?" Dr. Hartley asked.

"Yes. Definitely. Talking hasn't been a problem and I don't raise my voice."

"Good. I'd like you to continue seeing the vocal coach, and I'll see you again in six weeks." Her hesitant expression must have registered with him. "Is there a problem?"

She shook her head. "No, sorry. There's a chance I'll be back in Nashville by then."

"If you are, let my office know, and I'll send a referral. I know a couple of specialists in the area."

"Thank you. That'll be very nice. My plans are up in the air right now. I decided to buy a business in Lucky. I wasn't sure...." Her voice cracked, and her tears threatened. "I'm sorry."

He handed her a box of tissues. "No need to apologize. You've been through a lot. It's quite normal to be emotional."

"It's just... it's just" — she took a deep breath — "I thought I'd lost my singing voice completely."

Dr. Hartley smiled kindly. "Your vocal coach will know more about your range, but from where I sit, your larynx has been healing quite nicely. I won't be surprised to hear you're back to singing."

"Thank you..."

"Is there something else?"

"Well, actually, I'm thinking about singing at the fall festival in September. What do you think?"

"That's a fine idea."

"All right." She nodded. "Thanks again. I'll make the appointment and call your office if I need to cancel, depending on when I plan to go back to Nashville."

Megan spent the drive back home thinking.

The festival was still a month away. If she signed up to sing, she could concentrate on the renovations until then.

Excitement zinged through her over the renovation ahead. She happened to be meeting her favorite firefighter at Joe's Bar and Grill for supper so they could discuss more of her renovation ideas. She had so many plans for the building, and Chase was finally onboard.

No one was more surprised than she over her attitude change about Lucky. What she used to see as mundane she now saw as quaint. What she used to believe was busybody gossip she now saw as people caring enough to ask questions or offer advice out of concern.

Her stay in Lucky could have been horrible, but it didn't seem to be the same place she remembered as a teenager.

Or maybe Lucky hadn't changed as much as she had.

After dinner, she had a surprise planned for Chase. "I'm going to rock his world tonight," she murmured to herself. They'd both been busy. What with him coming off a forty-eight-hour shift, and her jobs, there'd been no time for intimacy.

She'd stopped at her favorite lingerie store on her way to her appointment and bought a little something sexy. The emphasis on little. Chase was going to love it.

A recognizable melody on the radio drew her out of her thoughts. "Honkytonk Angel."

She had another life waiting for her.

All evidence of her external bruises had disappeared weeks ago. So why didn't she feel the normal high when her song came on the radio? Thinking about her music career led her down a path she wasn't ready to go down and the inevitable choice she was going to have to make.

Instead, she'd focus on her new lingerie and her man.

Chase waited for Megan in front of Joe's. They planned to discuss the quote Ted the Tool had sent over. There was no doubt Megan planned to go through with this idea. He hated being at odds with her, so he was going to help her all he could. After all, this may be exactly what she needed to keep her in Lucky.

A nudge of guilt hit him. It was selfish to want to keep her here. It would have to be her decision. If she still could sing, he would never ask her to give up on her singing career.

That was first on his list. He wanted to know what the doctor said. If he hadn't still been on shift when she had to leave for the appointment, he would have taken her.

He could hear a difference in her voice. She sounded better to him, but he wasn't a doctor. The rasp was barely noticeable. He missed it. She had no idea what her sexy tone did to him.

Okay, knock it off.

Getting a boner on the sidewalk was the last thing he needed.

When Megan stepped out of her car, he headed her off. Taking her hand, he pulled her around the corner. Despite being in the heart of downtown, this provided a veil of privacy.

He had to touch her. He pulled her into his arms and kissed her deep and hard, pushing her up against the brick building, to position her just so. The kiss heated quickly, but then a loud whistle jolted them apart. He looked up in time to see Ryan Michaels driving past. The probie shouted, "Get a room."

Damn. Busted again.

Squeezing her arm, he said, "Sorry about that. I'll make sure Ryan knows to keep quiet." But he wasn't sorry. He wanted to kiss Megan anywhere and anytime.

"No, don't be sorry. That kiss was worth it." She smiled and took his hand.

He raised a brow. "Yeah, it was." He grinned. "I'm starving. How 'bout you?"

"Famished."

"Let's go, then."

They walked hand in hand down the sidewalk and across the street. Was Megan conscious of the fact that she was holding his hand in public? On Main Street, where anyone could pass? She was so relaxed.

There was a crowd at Joe's for a weeknight, but they found a booth.

Over the best burgers within a hundred miles, she told him what her doctor had said earlier.

"So, you should be able to get back to your singing. Does that mean you'll be heading back to Nashville soon?" He held his breath.

Please say no. Please say no.

"No," she said.

Chase released the breath he was holding.

She'd have to go back sometime. But he didn't like to think about that eventuality. It was too painful. He wasn't ready for it to all end. But he wouldn't stand in her way, either.

"I still have to work with the vocal coach some more." She swiped a fry in her ketchup, nibbling on it. "I'm going to stick around and get the business up and running."

He frowned. "I don't want to frighten you, but there's the matter of Sykes. He's still out there."

Megan's eyes shuttered, and she dipped her head down.

"Hey," he said, reaching across the table and tilting her face up. "We've got this. You're safe here. I only meant that until the cops get him. I'm glad you're staying here where I can protect you."

She nodded. "Thanks, Chase. You don't have to worry about that. I'm staying for at least another month to see to the renovation. Plus, there is the small matter of our marriage."

He nodded. "Any word from Rich? Has he settled on a plan yet?"

"No. But I'm sure he's working on something."

"Don't take this the wrong way. I'm not sure having our collective fates in his hands makes me less worried."

"I know what you mean." She cocked her head. "On the bright side, you're stuck with me."

A wicked grin spread across her face and made him fidget in his seat. Thankfully, the booth hid the hardening evidence.

She changed the subject, which helped his situation.

"Anyway, I want to get Espresso Yourself up and running. Hire a reliable staff."

"Espresso Yourself?" Chase raised a brow.

"Yep. What do you think?" Megan asked, but before he could respond, she continued, "It's the perfect name. A play on the fact that we're a coffee place, but with the addition I'm planning, that'll be where people can express themselves in other ways."

"Sounds good to me," he finally said.

Megan wiped her mouth. Set the napkin beside her plate that she had pushed to the side. She reached into her bag and pulled out paper and pencil. She was getting down to business.

He enjoyed watching her. She bubbled with excitement as she talked about her ideas. Over the weeks she'd been back, he'd seen her gradually get back to her enthusiastic, sparkling self. For that reason alone, he was grateful she'd come home with him. Of course, he was thrilled that their relationship was on a positive note, too.

"I have so many things I want to do with the building," she gushed.

Her hands and arms danced. "I'm going to freshen the awning over Bea's entrance, paint the flower boxes, and add a window box under the storefront window of the new building. I want them to match, of course, so it looks like it was always that way."

He would do whatever he needed to do to keep that smile on her face.

"I'm planning to paint the brick white. Then a huge rainbow on the exterior wall and I'll have Espresso Yourself stenciled below it." She held up her hands, bracketing her imagined design.

"Whoa. Slow down. Don't you think you might be getting a wee bit ahead of yourself?" He grinned.

"No, I don't. You must project your success. If I see it in my mind's eye, it will come true."

"First things first. Let's make a list of what we need to do. The guts before the glory, so to speak."

She frowned. "Isn't that what we're doing?"

"All right." He nodded toward her pad. "Let's make some notes. Do you have the quote from Reed?"

"Aye, aye, Captain." She saluted him before handing him the quote. Then she picked up her pen and held it over her notepad.

"Cute."

Megan gave him a cocky, fake smile.

He ignored her playfulness and studied the quote. It was fair. But he could save her some money by doing some of the work for her. If she wanted him to. He set the paper down and folded his hands on the table.

"Okay, so we'll do the standard fire inspection. As it sits now, I doubt the building will pass. But if you plan on doing new wiring, I don't think there will be an issue."

She jotted down what he said.

"What else do you see for the new space?" he asked.

"I want to build a platform to serve as a small stage for open mic night. Maybe put in a bar—I'm not sure about that. I could serve wine only. In either case, I'll need to apply for a liquor license."

"The other issue we'll have to investigate is handicap accessibility. New construction may force you to follow stricter codes," Chase said.

She took a sip of beer and nodded.

Finally, after an hour of discussion, they headed home. He paid their bill and escorted her across the street to her car.

"Thanks for dinner. Meet you at home," she said.

Hell, yes. Home. He loved to hear her refer to his home as her home. Their home.

She moved to open her door, but he blocked her efforts. "Hold on. I want to give you a goodbye kiss." He wrapped his arms around her and glanced around. "The coast is clear."

"Oh my gosh, Chase, it's like a five-minute drive to your house." She laughed.

"Five minutes too long," he said as he nuzzled her neck. His kisses played along her jawline, finally settling on her lips. He swept his tongue into her mouth, and she moaned and pressed up against him.

When they came up for air, she pushed away, opened the car door, and whispered, "Hold that thought, big boy."

Chapter 26

Megan beat Chase by a good ten minutes, since he had to walk over to the fire station to get his truck.

She took the fastest shower she'd ever taken, blew out her hair, and spritzed on her favorite fragrance. Champagne Cocktail. The new lavender-colored teddy fit like a glove. She lit candles and dimmed the lights. Satisfied with the setting, she laid on his bed and waited.

She heard the garage door and the jingle of Brady's collar as he greeted Chase.

"Megan?"

"Upstairs... already in bed," she yelled back.

"Umm, okay. I'll take Brady for a quick walk. Good night."

"Good night," she called down. She listened to the quiet of the night as she waited.

Emmie meandered into Chase's room, and Megan whispered, "Oh, no way, baby girl. Tonight, you are staying out of this room." She pointed to the door. "Out." Emmie glared at her, stiffened, and strutted back out of the room as if it had been her idea.

She heard him come back inside after the walk, and it sounded like he was passing through the rooms below, turning off lights and double-checking the doors. What if Chase decided to watch TV?

But Chase finally appeared in the doorway. A buzz of energy hit her. Pushing herself up on her elbows, she said, "Take your clothes off and get in this bed, now."

His eyes widened. A slow grin grew on his face. "Bossy. I like this side of your personality."

Laughing, she said, "Yeah, right. As long as I'm being bossy about something you want."

He nodded. "Of course. What's the magic word?"

Megan scooted closer, and grabbing his belt buckle, she gave him a hefty tug. He toppled onto her, and they laughed as they became entwined.

"Please."

Taking advantage of their position, he kissed her before she could say anything else. A slow, deep kiss and she pulled his shirt out of his pants, and he scrambled to unbutton it, yanking the sleeves down each arm.

She was wearing something new. At least he didn't remember seeing her in it. He pulled back and stared down at her, letting the sight of her leave an indelible impression in his mind. "God, you're even more beautiful than in my dreams." A flattering pink blush colored her cheeks.

"Is this new?" He traced a finger along the top of the bodice.

The sexy light purple nightie accentuated her breasts and long legs.

"Yep. I got it in Cleveland. She gasped as he pushed it aside to kiss her breasts. She unclasped the fabric, revealing her tantalizing breasts. He covered each with his hands. A perfect fit.

Chase nibbled down her neck to one, then the other breast. He played with her nipples with his fingers and used his tongue and teeth, which drew an instant squeal. He nibbled, licked, and sucked as he paid homage to her luscious breasts.

Soon, she was moaning and squirming beneath him.

Breathing hard, she said, "That feels incredible."

He deserted her breasts, traveling up the column of her pale neck. He inhaled her intoxicating fragrance as he pressed kisses along her jawline. "You taste and smell delicious."

"Mmm."

Finally, he captured another moan as he deepened the kiss, thrusting his tongue where it met hers.

Megan pulled her mouth away long enough to say, "I need you. Now."

He'd explode any second from his need for her. "Agreed." He made quick work of removing his pants and underwear. He opened the nightstand drawer and grabbed a condom.

"Here, let me," Megan said. She touched him, and he prayed the party wouldn't end before it even got started.

He pressed her onto her back. She was so beautiful, and he felt very lucky at that moment. He slid into her as he lowered himself and took her mouth in a slow kiss. Their bodies moved in sync with one another.

Once their breathing calmed, she asked, "So, do you like my new lingerie? Even if I only had it on for a few minutes.

"Yeah, it's sexy. But you always look great. You could wear a potato sack and be the sexiest woman in the room."

She laughed. "Thanks. I think." Stretching like a cat, she relaxed and curled into him, putting her head on his chest.

Yawning, she murmured, "That alarm clock is gonna ring early. Thanks for the dinner and your support. It means the world to me." Her voice getting quieter with each word. "You're the best guy."

She rolled to her side, and her last words were a sleepy murmur. "Love you, Chase." A soft, endearing snore followed.

Did she mean she loved him as a friend? Her brother's best friend, so her best friend? Or did she mean she loved, loved him?

He lay awake for a long time. Thinking.

<h1 style="text-align:center">Chapter 27</h1>

"You look like you're in a cheerful mood," Megan said to Chase when he stopped in the beanery to get a coffee a few days later.

"I am. I just got off the phone with Char Morgan. Her husband is doing well, and she plans to come back to work next week."

"That's good news."

But then why wasn't she as happy as Chase? Megan had gotten used to cooking for the guys. She'd grown fond of them and enjoyed being a part of something. She'd felt useful.

"Hey." Chase reached across the counter to tip her chin so he could get a better look. "What's going on in that pretty head of yours?"

She shook her head, pulling back so his hand dropped. "Nothing. I'm fine. I'm glad Tom is doing so well. I know you missed Char, and my cooking was only temporary. But I'll miss the guys." She shrugged.

He studied her for a moment. "I've got news for you. There is nothing temporary about you."

"Thank you for saying that." She squeezed his hand.

"It's true, and you can come by the station any time you want. The men will be happy to see you."

She turned back to the counter, straightening the impulse products. "This might be a sign."

"What kind of sign?"

"A *sign* sign. Like it was supposed to be. This will give me more time to focus on the building project and everything else I have going on."

He grinned. "Oh, that kind of sign."

"Oh you. Stop." She smacked his shoulder.

"I have to get back. Why don't you come out from behind that counter so I can give you a proper kiss goodbye?"

She shook her head, laughing. "There could be customers."

He glanced around. "I don't see any at the moment, do you?" He took several determined steps to the end of the counter. He cocked his head. "So, are you coming, or do I need to come back there?"

Giggling, she said, "Bossy much?" She walked out from behind the counter into his waiting arms. He pressed his lips against hers before completely enveloping her in his embrace. The kiss was hot. Her body tingled down to her core. She went up on her tiptoes, pressing herself even closer into him, and she heard him groan.

He broke the kiss and set her aside. "Sweetheart, you're dangerous. I need to get back to work. See you tomorrow afternoon when my shift ends."

"See ya, Captain Devine." She saluted and smiled to herself as he exited. Moving to the big storefront window, she watched as he headed down the street toward the fire station, stopping to say hello to a few folks along the way. She sighed, murmuring, "my very own superhero."

She looked across the street to the town square. They had made it a serene and beautiful spot to sit and watch the world go by. She was excited to get Espresso Yourself finished so it could add to the charm.

It was a sunny, warm afternoon, with people coming and going on the sidewalk. Megan spotted Becca James and her little girl Emma coming toward the café and waved.

The bell above the door jingled.

"Well, hello there." She squatted to Emma's level. "What brings you in today?"

"Mommy says we're having a girl's day out, and we're getting a treat."

"Is that so?"

Emma nodded vigorously.

Megan smiled. "What' would you like today?"

"Umm. Don't know. I love them all. What do you think, Mommy?"

Becca looked in the bakery case. "Hmm, what about the oatmeal raisin cookies?"

The cute little girl scrunched her face. "Mommy, you know chocolate is my favorite."

Becca and Megan laughed. "Yes, I know." She sighed and turned to Megan. "It can be a challenge finding a balance between being a mom and a doctor."

Megan nodded. "I get it. But as my grandma used to say, 'everything in moderation,' right?"

"I suppose so." Turning to Emma, Becca continued, " So, what'll it be?"

"A chocolate chip muffin. No, a brownie," Emma said as she eyed the bakery items in the case.

"The brownie is enormous. How 'bout we share it?"

Emma pouted. "Mommy."

"Emma." She stared right back at her daughter.

"Okaaaaay." The child didn't look thrilled by the prospect of having to share her chocolate treat.

"Why don't you go find a place to sit, Emma, while I get the brownie for you and your mom?" Megan asked.

She skipped to the table by the window and plopped into the seat, kicking her legs back and forth. Her excitement was contagious.

"How are you?" Becca asked as Megan warmed the brownie in the microwave.

"Fine. Probably better than fine. I'm good. The nightmares have almost gone away completely. The self-defense class and the therapy group have both been great. Both have very supportive women, that's for sure. Oh and, thanks for mentioning Dr. Winston to me."

"No problem. Glad it's going so well. Was that Chase I saw leaving ?"

"Yes." Megan squirmed. She had to remind herself this wasn't small-town gossip; Becca was her doctor and a friend.

"That's sweet that he came by to see you." She smiled. "He's such a hottie, isn't he? He reminds me of someone, but I can't think who."

Megan grinned. "Did you see any of the Fifty Shades movies?"

"Oh, my gosh." Becca snapped her fingers. "That's who he looks like—the guy who played Christian Grey. My. My." She fanned herself.

"I know, right?"

The two women giggled like schoolgirls who had found their brother's stash of porn.

Megan thought about how nice it was to have a genuine girlfriend. In Nashville, she had Brenda, but few others. It was difficult to see a person's true motives, which made making friends more challenging.

There was something about small towns. You pretty much knew who liked you and who didn't.

"Hey, have you heard anything about the fall festival?" Becca asked.

"Yeah, Actually, I'm considering singing."

Becca's eyes widened.

"Just one song," Megan quickly said. "And I need to clear it with my manager first. But I'm feeling stronger every day, and Dr. Hartley gave his approval and my vocal trainer thinks it will be an opportunity to get back onstage. One small step at a time." She shrugged.

"Well, I love the idea. As long as you feel ready."

Megan smiled. "Well, before I get up on any stage, I will have a few rehearsals. I don't want to disappoint any fans by flopping."

Her cell phone vibrated in her apron pocket. She looked at the name of the caller. "Speaking of the devil, it's my manager, Rich. Do you mind if I take this? I haven't spoken to him in a few weeks."

"No, not at all. We'll enjoy our brownie. I'll catch up with you later."

"Thanks," Megan said, then turned and answered. "Hey, Rich. How are you?"

"Fine. The question is, how are you?"

"I'm doing very well. Thank you."

"Okay, so when are you coming back to Nashville? We've gotten several calls for appearances in the area. People are eager to see you again."

"Really? That's good news, right?"

"Yes. So when can we expect to have you back in Nashville?"

"Well, I was going to call you. I'm considering performing a song at our fall festival in a few weeks."

"Festival? No, no, no. What about a contract? I'll need to speak to the organizer."

"Rich, I'm only talking about one song. And the organizer is an eighty-year-old hard-of-hearing couple. You will not get anywhere. Besides, if I do it, I'll be doing it for free. They can pass a hat or something. Even if they offer, I'd decline. I'd like to do it for the community. Everyone has been so kind to me here while I recuperated."

"Are you sure you're ready? If you flop, it could show up on Tik Tok."

"Gee, thanks for the vote of confidence, Rich."

"All right, but I want a note from your doctor telling me you're clear to sing."

"Oh my God, this isn't elementary school. You can take my word or not."

He sighed. "If you can do it without harming your voice, it could be a good way to bring you back. I can set up some publicity. Giving back to the community... that will play well in the press."

"Rich. "

"What? That's my job. Oh, and the whole marriage thing—"

"Wait. You should know things have changed between Chase and me. I'm not sure either of us wants to annul the marriage. Would it be so bad if we just said we got married two years ago and have kept it under wraps for our privacy?

"Two years? Really?"

"Well, I don't know. But I don't want to do anything yet. Can we wait awhile longer? Nothing has come out yet, right?"

"Not yet."

"Please, Rich."

"All right, all right. When is this festival, anyway?"

"The second weekend in September."

"Okay, let me know if you commit to it. Hey, my other line is ringing. Gotta go. Take care of yourself, kid."

Megan put her phone back in her pocket. Becca and her daughter had already gone, and the place was empty. She began cleaning up the counter.

She couldn't stop thinking about singing at the festival. Was it worth the risk? Ironically, it wasn't her voice that caused her the most concern. It was getting back on a stage that was causing her to question herself.

Was she ready?

Chapter 28

Somewhere off the grid...

Jason tossed and turned. His dream skirted the edges of a childhood nightmare. Locked in a small dark closet, he was hungry and afraid. The stale cigarette smell seeped from his mother's clothing, which hung listlessly above his head. How long had he been there? "Mama. Mama. Mama, please." But she never came.

He woke bathed in sweat, blinking until he got his bearings and remembered he was in a motel room somewhere in Iowa. He'd decided a long time ago he would never allow his fears to rule him because he was smarter than most people.

That's not true, is it? You still have nightmares. And you still have me in your head.

It was the sixth motel since leaving Nashville. He had been zigzagging across the Midwest to stay off the police's radar.

He was eager to see Megan. What was she doing? His curiosity got the best of him, so he called the studio, but they wouldn't give him any information. She could be anywhere. Frantic to find her, he had hacked into her manager's computer.

Bingo.

There was an email from Reynolds to Megan. He asked her how she was settling in and coping with living with her mother again.

What?

His mood was as erratic as the route he took. Fluctuating between wanting her to understand, it was all a misunderstanding and erupting into anger, blame, and revenge.

It was those feelings he harnessed to stay focused on the job ahead.

How dare she disrupt his entire life? Make him go on the run. She would pay.

She thought because she left Nashville, she could hide from him. She was stupid to think he couldn't find her wherever she might try to hide.

He headed east toward Ohio. He'd find her and teach her a lesson.

Chapter 29

Chase checked his watch. Time to take Brady for his evening stroll down to the lake and back. Every night, before dark, the two had their routine. Brady loved his walks and outdoor playtime.

Megan had a girl's night out with Becca and Lori Wilson, Becca's cousin. Romance Trivia over at the library, then to Joe's for drinks. Megan had accepted the invitation happily. It was great to see her enjoying herself. He hoped it was helping to make Lucky more than a temporary stop for her.

"Come on, Brady. Let's go."

Brady wagged his tail with his entire body. They stepped out onto the back patio and down the incline to the lawn. There was plenty of room for Brady to roam and sniff his favorite spots. He never strayed far.

Chase smelled smoke. Was someone burning leaves? That was dangerous, since it hadn't rained in weeks.

He scanned the horizon. He caught sight of black smoke billowing above the tree line across the lake. And where there was smoke... fire.

That had to be his parents' place. No one had purchased the lots on either side of their property, so their house was the only one that far down the road.

"Shit," he muttered. "Brady, come on, boy." He already had his phone in his hand, dialing 911 to report the fire. The guys would be here in less than ten minutes. But that might be too late.

He dialed his parents' landline. No answer. Chase put Brady inside and grabbed his keys.

"Stay. Good boy."

Jumping in his truck, he barreled down Lucky Lake Drive at a speed usually reserved for speeding tickets.

He tried his dad's cell. Dad answered on the fourth ring.

"Calling to argue about some—"

"Dad, are you home?" Chase's tone must have alarmed his father.

"No, I stayed late. I'm almost home. Why?"

"Is Mom home?"

"Yeah, she's got some sort of bug. Maybe the flu."

"She's been sick for a few days. I talked to her earlier. She was going to take some medicine to help her sleep. NyQuil or something. What's this about? What's going on?"

"I'm headed to your place now. I saw black smoke from my place."

"Shit. I'll be there in five minutes." The line went dead.

As Chase rounded the curve, he saw the flames.

He pulled up to the sprawling ranch-style house, praying the size of the house wouldn't hinder the search for his mom. He needed to find her fast.

He slammed on his brakes, making sure his truck wouldn't be blocking the fire truck. He grabbed the gear he kept in the utility bed of his truck for circumstances like this and assessed the situation as he suited up. There wasn't time to wait for the fire crew.

His dad's truck screeched to a halt next to him, and Dad jumped out and took off running toward the house. He didn't get more than a few yards before Chase grabbed his arm. "Dad, no. I got this."

"Your mom is in there. I'm going in."

"No, you're not. I will handle it. I'm trained for this."

His dad frowned and argued. "Look, Chase, this is my house."

Chase lost it. "Just once, one fucking time, can you cut your God damn bullshit? This is my job. Let me do it."

His dad blinked, took a step back, and nodded.

"Okay. Where should I look for Mom first? In your bedroom? Or the family room?"

"The bedroom, I guess. Yes, I'm sure of it. We had the family room painted last week, and the lingering paint fumes were giving her a headache. She'll be back in our room."

"Good. I'll go through the slider. You stay here. Let the crew know what's going on."

Chase had taken a few steps toward the house when his dad shouted, "Be careful, son."

His parents' bedroom was on the backside of the house, which he could reach via the deck. He could see his mom was lying on the bed. The slider was locked, so he pounded on the glass. But she didn't rouse. Was she unconscious, or had whatever cold medicine she'd taken knocked her out?

He used his Halligan bar to shatter the glass door.

Still, his mom didn't move. He reached in, unlocked the door, and raced to the bed. "Mom, wake up."

He shook her, but still no response.

Thick smoke billowed under the bedroom door, and he could hear the roar of the fire. Chase used every bit of his training to remain calm. He hauled her out of the bed, carrying her out of the house to the welcome sound of the siren.

When the truck stopped and the men jumped out, he yelled to the EMT, "She's unconscious."

The EMT grabbed a bag and hauled ass over to where Chase laid his mother on the lawn. "I don't know if it was the smoke or a cold medicine she took that knocked her out."

His dad rushed over. "Oh, Patsy, thank God."

"Dad, let him do his job." But Chase didn't wait around to see if his father listened. He was already moving toward the front of the house to support his men.

"Anyone else in the house?" he heard someone yell.

He turned back to his dad. "Anyone else in the house?"

Dad shook his head. "No," he relayed to the crew. "Only my mom."

Thank God he'd smelled the smoke when he had. He knew only too well how quickly a fire could spread. He didn't want to think about what could have happened.

"Captain, we got this. Go be with your folks."

Extinguishing the fire took over an hour. The kitchen and laundry room got hit the hardest. There was a lot of smoke and water damage even where the fire hadn't burned. What a mess. The design of the house kept the kitchen and family room on one side of the grand living and dining room, the bedrooms on the other.

That design may have saved his mother's life.

Turned out, his mom had taken a little extra night-time cold syrup, and it knocked her out. They were going to keep her overnight at the hospital for observation because she was coughing. But the medical team thought the smoke inhalation was minimal.

When he entered her room, his parents exchanged an awkward look. Chase cleared his throat. "How are you feeling? I just wanted to check on you before I head home."

"Oh, Chase. Thank you. You saved my life."

He nodded, but cocked his head. "Of course. It's my job."

A tear dripped onto her cheek. Shit, he hated tears.

"I know." She looked over at Dad. "I know we haven't been supportive. We never understood why you do what you do until now." She sniffed.

What could he say? It was true. But he didn't want to point that out. She needed to rest. Dad rose from the chair beside her bed. Extended his hand. "Thank you, Chase."

A strong, solid handshake ended with his dad pulling him in to pat him on the back. "I'm sorry for all the times I've made you feel you shouldn't be doing what you do. Your mom and I... well, after Conner died, we just wanted to protect you. I thought if I could get you to come work at Devine Construction, you'd be safe."

"Dad, I could fall off a roof and break my neck or get into a car accident like Conner. There are no guarantees in life. I'd rather do what I love for as long as I can."

"I think we have a better understanding now, and we'll be more supportive of your choice from now on, but promise us you'll always be careful."

Chase nodded. "Of course. I better get going. I told Megan I'd be home by midnight. "He stopped at the door and turned. "I'm sorry about the house. I wish we could have saved more of it."

"It's just a house," said Dad.

"Good thing you know a reputable contractor, huh?" Chase halfheartedly said.

His parents smiled. "Good night," they said in unison.

Was it too much to hope that his parents finally understood and accepted his decision to be a firefighter?

Chapter 30

The lazy days of summer rolled into the fall as Chase and Megan fell into a comfortable routine.

Megan threw Bea a retirement/going-away party, and the renovation project was in full swing by mid- September. She spent most of her days over at Espresso Yourself, ensuring that her vision was on track.

"What do you think of this shade of blue?" she asked Chase one evening when they were working side by side on the second floor.

"It's blue."

She rolled her eyes. "Yes, I know it's blue—so are these other ones." She pointed to the other five paint samples.

He shrugged. "What do you want me to say? Blue is blue."

"Look at these shades and tell me you really can't see the differences."

He smirked.

"Oh, you're so not funny. Stop it and help me decide."

"Okay, this one." He pointed to the one that had a little purple hue in it. "It reminds me of the color the sky gets at sunset over the lake."

"I like that one, too." She smiled.

"That's a good thing, right?" he teased.

"Yes, it is. Now come over here and kiss me."

"You don't need to ask me twice. I've been hoping we'd finish up soon so we could neck for a while."

"I might be able to offer you a bit more than necking."

"You've got my undivided attention."

"Thought so." She motioned with her pointer finger. "Follow me."

Megan's office was one of the first rooms the crew had finished, and she'd moved some furniture in yesterday, including a very soft and comfy sofa she'd gotten from Bea, who'd had lots of furniture she wanted to get rid of before the move.

Megan flipped the light switch on and shouted, "Surprise."

"Oh, wow. This is great."

Pride and happiness bubbled inside her. The office was small, but it'd suit her needs. The fact that one room was completed made her feel like the end was in sight.

"I thought you'd like to help me test out the sofa. Interested?"

"You know I am." He pulled her down beside him, and she collapsed on his lap. Chase nuzzled her neck, tickling her until she giggled.

But their light, playful kisses soon turned to heated ones. Chase raised his head. "I'd like to take this further, but I'd prefer the comfort of our bed than this sofa. It's nice, don't get me wrong, but —"

"Oh, yeah, I forget you're getting old."

"Ha. Meet me at home, and I'll show you just how young I still am."

"I like that idea. Okay, go home and take care of Brady and feed Emmie, too, please. I'll lock up here. I should be about fifteen minutes behind you."

"Sounds like a plan."

He reached for her and pulled her up against his hard muscles. She squeezed his sinewy arms and kissed his mouth. A slow, delicious kiss that promised more.

"Keep that up and I'll change my mind about the bed."

She laughed. "Go." She shooed him.

One last quick peck and he headed for the door.

"Oh, wait. Will you take this box for me?" She pointed to a box on the floor. "We're handing fliers out at the festival this weekend. The Fall Harvest Festival will be a great place to promote Espresso Yourself."

"Sure. You want me to put them in your car or my truck?"

"It doesn't matter. I can switch them at the house later. It's just one less thing for me to carry home tonight."

"Got it. See you in a few, babe."

She couldn't remember when he started calling her babe. He didn't do it often, but it was sweet.

"Aye, aye, Cap," she replied.

Megan finished up a few final touches, but as she locked up the building, a chill ran down her spine. She whipped around, searching the street and the surrounding area. Seeing no one, she shook it off. But this was how she'd felt and how her body had responded when she sensed she was being watched before.

"Stop it," she reprimanded herself.

The next day, Chase waited in front of Joe's for Megan to meet him for lunch. When he saw her come out of Espresso Yourself, a warm feeling came over him. He loved her. He had for a long while.

It was past time he told her. It was also time to talk about their marriage. He needed to be honest with her. He didn't want a divorce. Or an annulment.

He wanted to remarry this woman in a beautiful ceremony in front of family and friends. They would have to work through all the details, but it could work.

Right?

"Chase." She waved. He turned and smiled.

"How's your day so far?" he asked, pulling her into an embrace. He glanced around before he covered her mouth with a kiss. When they finally broke apart, she said,

"It just got a whole lot better."

"Hmm. I have an idea," he said.

"Uh-oh. Sometimes your ideas are crazy."

"I don't know. You might like this one."

She cocked her head and grinned. "I'm listening."

"Why don't we skip Joe's? I'm thinking nooner." He air quoted. "We can stop at the deli and pick up a couple of sandwiches."

She bit her bottom lip, as she often did. "It's not that I hate the idea." She smiled up at him. "You know I don't. But there are still some things I need to get done before tomorrow."

"Tell you what—after lunch, I'll come back with you, and I'll be at your command the rest of the day."

"Really?"

"Yep, I have the rest of the day off. There's nothing I'd rather do than spend it with my girl."

"Wow, that's too good to be true. What if I want you to be my sex slave?"

He chuckled. "Babe, willing and able. Just sign me up. You've had me wrapped around your pinkie from the moment you moved in with me. Don't you know that?"

She pinched his cheek. "Always good to hear." A sexy smirk escaped her lips. "Beat you to your truck." Megan took off running.

He let her beat him because he was already a winner.

As it turned out, their lunch plan got interrupted when Chase got an emergency call from the fire station. There was a fire at the hospital, and they needed all hands on deck. He dropped Megan off at Espresso Yourself before heading straight to the hospital to meet the team.

On Saturday, the excitement for the Fall Harvest Festival bubbled out of Megan. Or was that nervous energy?

The meteorologist on the local news promised perfect weather. Cooler but sunny—the type of weather one prayed for when hosting an outdoor event in September.

Vendors from all over the surrounding areas brought their wares to sell in booths set up in the town square. The regular farmer's market tripled in size that weekend.

The PTO had set up a table for their bake sale, and each year, the best bakers in town competed for a blue ribbon in the pie contest.

The festivities continued across the street and down a block at Four-leaf Clover Community Park. There were arts and craft tables, games, and pony rides for the kids. Carnival food trucks lined up along the street that ran parallel to the park.

Apple cider, donuts, hot dogs, and slushies were all represented and there was already a line forming at the truck that sold caramel apples and elephant ears.

Around noon, Brenda showed up at the park and surprised Megan.

"Oh, my gosh. What are you doing here?" The two women hugged.

"Chase called me. I'm here to enjoy a few days on Lucky Lake, kicked off by hearing my favorite Nashville star sing."

"Oh, Chase didn't say a word."

Brenda shook her head. "Well, duh, he intended it as a surprise."

"It certainly is a surprise. A wonderful one."

"He might have also thought you could use a little more moral support as you take the stage again." She cocked her head.

Wow, Chase could certainly read her. Though her rehearsal went off without a hitch, she still hadn't been in front of a live audience in months.

Hopefully, it was like riding a bike.

Brenda's eyes narrowed. She had seen all of Megan's pre-show meltdowns. Nothing prima donnish. Simple nerves that could take away someone's self-confidence.

"I'm fine. I am. I'm not nervous about singing to this audience. It's filled with old and new friends and neighbors. People who care about my well-being. There's no pressure at all. Right?"

Her friend nodded. "Good for you. I'm happy for you. And I'm very proud of the progress you've made. You hung in there. That's what matters." Brenda hugged her again.

"Chase is taking a turn at the dunk tank. Let's go check it out, since it's just over there." Megan pointed to the other side of the park.

Sure enough, he was sitting on the perch aloft the tank of water, ready to take a plunge. He was still dry, but there was a line waiting for their chance to dunk her dreamy Captain Devine.

She recognized some men from the fire station. Brave souls who weren't worried about retaliation from their superior. She laughed when Kell stepped up.

He wound up.

The pitch was good.

SPLASH.

She was close enough to hear Chase's exasperated response. "Payback, buddy. Payback."

Kell laughed. "You can try. Who made all-district senior year?"

"Yeah, yeah, whatever." Good sport that he was, Chase climbed back up, winking at her.

She squirmed, heat spreading down to her core.

Thankfully, no one could see what that simple little wink, with its promise of things to come, did to her. She stepped closer to him and asked, "You think you'll be dry in time for my song?"

He cocked his head and smirked. "Will you?"

Despite the blush she felt creep up her neck, she rolled her eyes at him, then turned back to her friend. "Hey, are you hungry?" Megan asked Brenda.

"Starved." They both laughed because that was always Brenda's response.

"Come on. Let's walk over to my place. I can't wait to show you Espresso Yourself."

❦

At dusk, people lined up their lawn chairs to relax after the day of fun activities. Entertainers would start performing on the temporary mini stage soon.

At her suggestion, the festival committee passed a hat for donations to the Survivors of Violence, a nonprofit that Megan started to support other victims of violence who needed a safe place to live, counseling, and help with medical bills.

Megan sang "Honkytonk Angel," which brought on raucous applause.

She wanted to give the audience something that called for a generous freewill offering, but she didn't want to upstage the other performers. Plus, she committed herself to only the one song. She took a bow and exited stage left.

Mom, David, Kell, Brenda, and Chase, of course, were in the front row, and instead of peering into the dark for the crowd, she could see faces in the dusk. The only person missing was Becca. There may have been an emergency that kept her from coming.

Chase had the biggest smile on his handsome face and something else. Was that love in his eyes? He had been on the brink of telling her something when he got the call about the hospital fire.

Preoccupied with her thoughts, she stepped off the makeshift stage and bumped into a man. "Excuse me, I'm so—" Something hard jammed into her ribs. She turned to look at the person.

Jason.

Megan gasped, and her body shook. Scenes from every nightmare she'd had about him raced through her mind as his grip bit into her arm.

"Hello, Megan. Don't scream or make a scene. This is a gun." He jabbed her again to make his point. "And I'm not afraid to use it."

Her breath quickened, and her heartbeat pounded in her chest.

Think. Focus. Do not panic.

He pulled her up against him, his hot breath on her neck sending a shiver down her spine.

"Finally, Megan. I've missed you. Walk. Nice and slow."

"Jason," she choked out. "I have family... friends... here."

"Better hope they stay back. Now move."

He pushed her along in front of him. He had a slight limp, but it didn't seem to slow him down.

They had to maneuver through the people milling around the stage. He was moving toward the street.

When he had to dodge a large group, she stumbled. But he hauled her back up, tightened his grip, and continued.

You can't let him take you anywhere.

People noticed when she didn't respond to their congratulatory comments and the few autograph requests.

Please, please someone call the cops. Find Chase and Kell.

Just then, John and Margie McHale, owners of Big John's Sporting Goods store on Main, stalled their movement. John put his hand out to shake and said, "Hey, great concert."

"Nod nice and friendly," Jason whispered, his spittle hitting her ear, and she had to choke back the nausea.

John McHale frowned when she didn't reply to his comment immediately. "Is everything all right?"

Jason jabbed her again. "Ow." She tried to cover by quickly saying, "I'm glad you enjoyed the show." *Now or never.*

She rushed to continue, "Let Chase know a friend from Nashville—" The butt of the gun dug into a rib. The nausea threatened again, and she doubled over in pain.

John McHale took a step closer. "Is this guy hurting you?"

She shook her head. "No." A lunatic like Sykes wouldn't think twice about shooting an old man. She stumbled again when Sykes pushed her to continue walking.

Chapter 31

Chase strolled toward the area beside the stage, ready to congratulate his Nashville star. She rocked the stage tonight. He grinned when he remembered how she had embraced the energy of Las Vegas.

She'd strapped it on like he did his forty-five pounds of fire gear. Ready for whatever came her way. That's how she performed. She gave her all. She owned the stage. He couldn't be prouder.

Performing was who she was. How could he ask her to stay in Lucky?

There are those doubts again.

He pushed the negativity aside. This wasn't the time or place. But soon he was going to have to face reality.

Kell leaned in to be heard over the crowd. "You okay, buddy?" But before Chase could answer, John McHale jogged up to them, Margie trailing behind him by a few steps. The old man was out of breath.

"Whoa, John, everything all right?" Chase asked.

John shook his head. "No, I don't think so. It's Megan."

The hair on Chase's arms and neck stood up. "What about Megan?"

"We saw her over there." He pointed to the other side of the stage. "She was with a man and I could tell she was scared. She said, 'Tell Chase a friend from Nashville...' but then she just stopped talking. It was like she got cut off. The man she was with did not look friendly. I think he was hurting her."

Chase looked at Kell. "Sykes."

"Where did you see her?" Kell asked.

John pointed again. "Heading toward the cars parked along the street.

"John, do you have a cellphone?"

The old man nodded.

"Call 911," Chase said, then took off at a run with Kell, right beside him, searching the crowd for Megan.

"There." Kell pointed.

When they were within ten feet, Chase shouted, "Megan!"

Sykes flipped around to see who shouted her name.

"Chase, Kell," she gasped. "He has a gun."

The people in the immediate area heard the word gun. Screams and frantic movement broke out, creating chaos all around them.

"Chase, you keep his attention. I'll flank him. Maybe with all this commotion, he won't notice."

Chase nodded. "Sykes. Let her go. You can't escape. The cops will have this place surrounded in minutes."

Sykes continued walking backward, dragging Megan with him. Kell dodged around the bystanders. Chase was torn between telling the crowd to run for cover and keeping them in place to hide Kell's efforts to get behind the asshole.

He got close enough to hear Sykes say, "Another boyfriend? You really are a slut."

"No, that's my brother," she cried.

Chase fisted his hands.

Kell was inching closer.

"Stay back. I'll shoot." Sykes waved the gun.

There were more screams of panic and pushing and shoving to get to safety. The pandemonium worked to their advantage. Kell was able to move in behind Sykes and Megan.

"I won't let you take my sister."

Sykes whipped around, dragging Megan, causing her to stumble again.

"Megan, are you okay?" Chase shouted.

"Just rosy," she yelled back.

What the hell? Rosy? She was clearly not rosy. This wasn't the time for sarcasm. She looked terrified. Then it clicked. When she was a little kid, he and Kell taught her that if she was ever being held by a bully at school, she should collapse to the ground unexpectedly. "Ring around the rosy, a pocket full of posies. Ashes, ashes, we all fall down." *Good girl.*

Kell's expression never changed but for an infinitesimal nod of his head. Chase reciprocated.

Timing was everything. They didn't want that gun going off and injuring anyone. Especially Megan.

Kell inched another step. Chase inched another step.

Sykes turned to see Kell moving in on them. "Stay back. I swear I'll shoot."

"Here's the thing: I spent twelve years in the Marines, facing the nastiest of the nasty in the Middle East. You think that little handgun scares me? It'll take a lot more than that to take me down."

Suddenly, Megan stomped on Sykes's foot and fell limply to the ground.

Kell charged.

Chase moved in quickly, kicking the man in the back of his knee to knock him off balance.

The gun went off. Someone grunted.

Kell lifted Sykes off the ground and pummeled him. "I told you that gun wouldn't stop me. You son of a bitch." Sykes collapsed to the ground.

Chase pulled Megan up from the ground and into his arms. "It's over. You're safe." He kissed her forehead quickly and wrapped his arms around her, holding her close. She trembled, but held tight. "I've got you," Chase said.

Kell stood over Sykes with his foot on the man's back. Blood pooled on Kell's left shoulder.

"You're hurt. We need to call an ambulance," Megan said.

"Don't worry. It's just a scratch. Bullet just grazed me."

The next thirty minutes were a blur. Sheriff Andrews and his men arrived and took a bruised and battered Jason Sykes into custody. The paramedics patched Kell up. He'd live.

Chase hadn't let go of Megan the entire time the cops talked to her. Her body still trembled.

"Wow, I'm impressed you remembered the *Ring Around the Rosie* trick," said Kell.

"Yeah, that was awesome," Chase added.

"Hey, I'm not completely helpless. I've been taking self-defense classes, too, you know." They were all silent for a moment, then she continued, "But I don't know how it would have turned out if you two hadn't been here. Thank you."

Not one for a lot of sentiment, Kell said, "So, is this how all your concerts end?"

"More or less." She grinned. "You're so not funny."

The two men laughed. When Megan chuckled, she felt a stab if pain. "Ouch."

The paramedics took a quick look at her after they bandaged Kell's left shoulder. They wanted her to get an x- ray, and Chase offered to drive her.

The cops had cordoned off the area by the ambulance. Finally, they allowed Ruby and Brenda access, and the two women rushed over.

"Thank you, boys, for keeping my little girl safe," said Ruby.

Megan bristled. "Mom, I'm not helpless."

Chase spoke up. "Actually, Ruby, Megan saved herself. We were there for the assist, but she came up with the idea."

Megan squeezed his hand and mouthed, "Thanks."

He winked at her.

"My goodness." Ruby hugged Megan. "If I'd known my baby girl could kick a man's ass like that, I never would've sent Chase to Las Vegas to keep an eye on you. I was just so worried about you when you went out there for that contest."

Fuck.

Megan's eyes went wide and her jaw dropped. Then those green eyes narrowed to slits directed at Chase.

The blood drained from his face, and the noose tightened around his neck. His world crumbled.

Can't build on lies.

Megan pulled away from him. "What's she talking about, Chase? I thought you went to Vegas for a convention."

He frowned. "No, I never actually said that."

"Oh, my God. It's true, isn't it? It was all a setup. My mom sent you to... what? Babysit me? None of it was real."

He shook his head vehemently. "No. It was real."

"Our wedding. The sex. How did that fit into the plan? Was that all you were after?"

"What? No. Of course not."

The others listened to the exchange.

"Wedding?" Ruby asked.

"Sex?" Kell asked.

Everyone began talking over one another.

"How old were you?" Kell asked.

"What about a wedding?" Ruby asked.

She glared at her brother. "It doesn't matter. That's not what's important."

"The hell it isn't."

"What wedding?" Ruby asked again. Clearly, she focused on only that.

"Mom, will you stop? Leave it alone."

"Look, Megan, we really need to talk," Chase said, his voice sounding like a whine to his ears. Yeah, he actually whined, for fuck's sake.

She threw her hands up. "Oh no. The time to talk is long past. You could have talked when I woke up in your bed. Or when I asked you about the marriage certificate, I knew nothing about. Or, hey, here's a thought. Maybe you could have said something in the four months we've been living together."

"Living together?" Mom asked.

She ignored her mom.

"Brenda, will you take me over to the hospital?" Brenda nodded, and the two women marched off.

Chase turned just as Kell's fist landed a punch to his face. "Fuck. That hurt." He rubbed his jaw. "What'd you do that for?" Chase glared at Kell, who glared right back.

"You had sex with my baby sister."

"Oh, for God's sake. First, she was like twenty-two. Hardly a baby. Second, she was my wife."

That shut Kell up for the moment. Turning to Ruby, Chase said, "With all due respect, Ruby, you have shitty timing."

"What? I had no idea Megan didn't know the truth. Seems like you're the one with shitty timing."

"How do we know you didn't pressure her?" Kell asked.

"I guess you'll have to take my word as your oldest friend. But I won't go into any details with you or anyone else. What happened between Megan and me in Vegas was between us. We were both adults."

Chase would never divulge the truth surrounding that night. A lot of alcohol had blurred their judgment. No one needed to know that.

He combed his fingers through his hair. "I don't have time for this. I gotta talk to Megan." He stalked toward his truck. With any luck, he'd catch up to her and could explain.

But could he? Why hadn't he told her?

He missed her at the hospital, and when he got home, she was gone. She'd left a note scribbled on a napkin on the kitchen counter.

I'm staying with Brenda. Took Emmie.

That was it? No further explanation or sign that she was willing to talk.

"I thought Brenda was staying here," he muttered to Brady when the dog came into the kitchen, doing his best imitation of Eeyore. He stared at Chase with his sad, brown doggie eyes.

"Not you, too. I know I screwed up. I don't need you to pile on the guilt." As if the dog understood, he pushed his head between Chase's knees, wanting to give and receive comfort. Chase patted the dog. "I know, buddy. I know. It's quiet. But we'll figure it out."

Chapter 32

Megan packed a bag and stayed with Brenda at the bed & breakfast. Brenda was a shoulder to cry on her while keeping her opinions and advice to herself.

Unlike Mom and Kell, who had always offered far too many opinions. They meant well, but this was something Megan would have to figure out on her own.

The nightmares returned, and she was frustrated that the creep had shaken her confidence all over again. At least he was now behind bars where he belonged.

Her emotions were raw. As freaked out as she was over Sykes, it was the hurt and anger over Chase's betrayal that tore through her. Chase had lied. Again.

How had she allowed herself to fall in love with him? He obviously didn't respect or understand her. He knew that her mother's manipulations and controlling tendencies were a part of what drove Megan away from Lucky in the first place.

How could she ever trust him again?

Mom was completely out of line, too. How could she send Chase to babysit her? Megan felt mortified.

She couldn't decide what to do. Staying in Lucky seemed out of the question. She couldn't face seeing Chase, but running into him was bound to happen. She simply wasn't ready to talk to him until she had time to build up her mental strength first.

But could she leave behind everything she'd been working so hard on here?

"A pushy real estate developer, Bill Duffy, I think was his name, contacted me about selling the two buildings to him," Megan said over breakfast in the quaint dining room. Lilac season was long past, but there were still plenty of lilacs. These were of the fake, store-bought variety. Pretty just the same.

"That seems aggressive to me. I mean, where did he get the idea that you'd even want to sell?"

"I don't know. Maybe he assumed I wouldn't stick around. I'm sure the grapevine has been busy. The guy was annoying and smug. I didn't like the vibe I got from him. Or maybe I'm not in the frame of mind to deal with his bullshit. If I sell, it won't be to him."

"You've just come through a traumatic situation. Don't be hasty. You don't have to sell, nor do you have to move back to Nashville.

Basically, you don't need to decide right now," Brenda said. "Give yourself some time." She released Megan's hand to sip her tea.

Megan shook her head. "Without Chase, what's keeping me here? They arrested Sykes, so I don't have to stay away from Nashville in fear of him. Don't you think I need to make a clean break?"

Brenda reached over to stop Megan from moving the food around on her plate. "At the risk of sounding like your mom, you have to eat something."

"I know. Though, I'm afraid I won't be able to keep it down. Some people eat their feelings, and others can't eat a thing during stressful times." She shrugged. "I'll drink a smoothie later."

"All right. But I'll be checking."

"What would I do without you?" Megan laughed weakly. "Don't answer that. I never want to find out."

Later, Megan called an old family friend, Bruce Kincaid, who was now a realtor, to ask his advice. After the preliminary polite chitchat, she explained what she wanted to do about her properties.

"So, you're telling me not to sell it? I'm not sure you understand how this process works." Bruce chuckled.

"I know it's odd. If I decide to sell, I'll use you for sure. That pushy real estate developer really put me off."

"No worries. I'll handle it."

"Appreciate it."

"Hey, I heard what happened at the festival," Bruce said. "I'm glad you weren't hurt."

"You and me both. Listen, I've got to run. I've got some packing to get done."

Bruce whistled. "Wow, Devine really screwed up, huh?"

"I'm sure the town gossips are having fun with this."

His tone sobered. "No one enjoys seeing the two of you unhappy."

She needed to change the subject before she cracked. "Thank you for your help."

✤

She was gone. Gone, gone. As in left town gone. How could he fix the problem if she wasn't there? And she refused to respond to his text messages or phone calls.

He'd called Brenda once—okay, three times— simply to ask how Megan was doing. He was worried about her. After what she went through on Saturday night, her welfare was his first concern. But he had a lot of groveling and explaining to do. He didn't care if he seemed desperate, because that was exactly what he was.

"Captain?"

"Hmm. Sorry, Michaels. I didn't hear you. I'm wrapped up in getting the schedule done." He lifted the paperwork as exhibit A.

Bullshit.

Megan was all he was thinking about.

The probie continued, "Sir, we were thinking." He gestured to the other men. "Sorry to be so blunt, but you messed up with Megan. If you don't mind a little advice..." Michaels surveyed the group of men sitting around the TV. They all nodded in encouragement.

Shit. Was there anyone in this town who doesn't know I fucked up?

Apparently, even his men had been discussing his relationship.

Chase arched his brow. But hell, he was desperate, so he'd listen to advice from anyone at this point. "Sure. Why not? Lay it on me." He laid the pen and schedule down on the table.

"We think you need a grand gesture." Michaels looked uncomfortable and kept glancing over to his buddies for moral support. "We, the guys, and I, think you need to do something special, something big to win Megan back. We're all real fond of her."

As if he wasn't aware of that.

What are the specifics of this advice? What do you guys suggest?"

Another probie, Chad Ross, jumped up and came over to the table. "Sir, you know her better than anyone. You'll think of something special." He cleared his throat. "It might mean you have to go down to Nashville."

Michaels and Ross meant well.

"I'll take it under advisement. For now, I want the trucks and your gear inspected." When no one moved, he barked, "Move it." They hurried out of the lounge.

Char, who was prepping for the next meal, had been silent through the discussion. Now she tsked loud enough for Chase to hear.

He looked over his shoulder. "Was that in sympathy or disapproval?"

"As long as you're in the mood for receiving advice, I've got some, too." She walked around the counter and sat next to him.

At least Char might know what she was talking about. She and Tom had celebrated their sixtieth last spring. "You're not going to take no for an answer. So, yes, by all means, give me some advice. I'm drowning here."

She patted his hand. "The grand gesture idea is a good one. Give that some thought. I'm sure you can think of something unique and meaningful just for her."

He nodded.

"But that's not the answer," she said.

"It's not?"

She shook her head. "No, you'll win Megan's heart back with five magical words."

He sat up straighter, leaning in toward Char. "What words?"

"The most important thing, before anything else, you need to apologize. You need to say, 'I'm sorry' and mean it. Too many men are afraid to admit when they make a mistake. Women need to hear those words. I'm sure Megan does. If you're sorry for the heartache you caused her, you need to tell her."

He nodded his understanding. "You said five words. That's only two."

A wistful smile played on Char's face. "Chase, you need to tell her you love her, especially if you haven't said it to her before. Say 'I love you.'"

Had he? He showed her by loving her. But that wasn't quite the same thing. Sex had never been a problem between them.

"Tom and I never go to sleep mad. Why would we when it's so much fun making up?" She waggled her brows.

"Ugh, Char. You're like my grandma. Let's keep the details private."

She laughed. "Oh, I thought your generation was free and easy. Nothing to be embarrassed about."

Yeah, right.

"Thanks, Char."

"You two deserve your happily ever after. You just need to get her on the same page."

❧

The next day, Lucky's grapevine was alive with news. Bruce Kincaid was overseeing the sale of Espresso Yourself. Chase was shocked she put it on the market.

If it was the last thing he did, he'd win her back. And when she was back, she'd want her brick baby waiting for her. Espresso Yourself had become her new dream. She had so many cool ideas to make the space alive again. It had to have hurt for her to walk away.

Maybe there was something he could do.

In a rash decision, he called Bruce to put in an offer. "I heard you really screwed up." The realtor couldn't resist adding his personal two cents before moving on to business. And the irony wasn't lost on Chase. Megan had always hated the gossip of the small town. It was her biggest complaint. And now half the town knew their business.

"You heard right. But I'm trying to make it up to her. I want to buy the store for her. I don't want her to know it's me, though. Can you work that out?"

Is that grand enough?

"Here's the thing, she didn't put it on the market. She just wanted me to let her know if there is any interest. I could let her know I have a very interested buyer."

"That will work. I want to surprise her. I guess it all hinges on whether she forgives my ass and wants to come back to Lucky. If not, I'm prepared to move to Nashville. Then you can add my house to your listings.

Chase could shift the schedule around so he could take some time off. Now he just needed to talk to Kell. Clear the air.

Kell agreed to stay at the house to take care of Brady. When Kell arrived, Chase said, "Hey, man, thanks again for agreeing to be roomies with Brady." Upon hearing his name, Brady nuzzled into Chase. "Yeah, boy, Kell is going to take good care of you."

"Sure am. Brady and I have a date on your boat, don't we, boy?" Brady deserted Chase for the other sweet talker.

"Look Kell, I feel like I need to set you straight on a few things."

Kell raised a brow. "Can I get a beer first?"

Handing Kell his beer, Chase said, "I want you to know how guilty I felt about what happened in Vegas. For a long time, I felt like I let you down. But the truth is, I didn't need you to ask me to watch over Megan. I would have done it, anyway.

"At the risk of you punching me again, I gotta tell you I noticed Megan when she was seventeen. She was home from college when Connor died. Her maturity, her kindness and big heart blew me away. Chase ran his hand through his hair. "I avoided her out of respect for you and, of course, the fact that she was still underage.

"I kept tabs on her through the following years, then when Ruby asked me to go to Vegas ... well, she didn't have to twist my arm. Megan was twenty-two. And there was an instant mutual attraction. There was never any doubt that Megan and I got together because we both wanted it."

Kell held his hand up. "Okay, I get the picture."

"Are we good?"

"Yeah, I wouldn't be here otherwise. She's my baby sister, but it's obvious you care about her."

Chase nodded. "I love her. I had feelings for her before, but when she came back home, everything became clear."

"Well, I don't envy you. Talking sense into that sister of mine will be a challenge."

"Yeah, I know. But it'll be worth it. I'm miserable. Nothing makes sense without her sassy mouth telling me what I think." He shrugged.

Kell laughed. "Good luck."

"Thanks. I'm going to need it, I'm afraid."

"See you in a few days," Kell said.

The two gave each other a quick man hug and pat on the back. Chase gave Brady a quick pat on his head.

"Bye, Brady, be a good boy."

Chapter 33

In the week Megan had been back in Nashville, she hadn't contacted Rich. Or gone into the studio. She'd been holed up at Brenda's place, licking her proverbial wounds. She needed to stop moping around and move on, but it just wasn't happening.

"How 'bout we get dressed up tonight and go out on the town?" Brenda suggested when she walked into the kitchen where Megan sat nursing her glass of wine. At her feet, Emmie meowed.

"Nah, I don't think so. Not feeling it."

Brenda's eyes narrowed. "Well, the bathrobe over sweats is a nice look, too."

"Ha, ha."

Brenda glanced at the clock. "Have you eaten anything, or are you on a liquid diet?"

Megan raised the glass. "It's five o'clock somewhere." Shrugging, she took another sip.

Brenda stared until Megan squirmed. "I'm sorry. Have I been awful to live with?" she asked.

"No. I'm here for you. Of course, you aren't going to get over your broken heart in a couple of days. But it might make you feel better if you shower and dress."

"You're right. I need to get over myself, huh?"

"That's not what I'm saying at all. Take all the time you need. I'm here if you need me," Brenda offered.

"The last six months have been harrowing. Even when you weren't in Nashville, there was always the worry that Sykes was still out there somewhere. Cut yourself some slack. You just might want to get out of your bathrobe." She smiled.

Later, after Megan had showered, brushed her teeth, and applied some makeup, she felt fractionally human again.

"Don't you feel 100 percent better now?" Brenda said cheerfully.

"Maybe 85 percent." She winked at Brenda. "Thanks for the gentle push."

"What are friends for? Hey, listen, would you mind if I run a few errands?" Brenda asked.

What a strange question.

"Since when do you need my permission to run errands?" Megan scoffed.

"I don't, but I wanted to make sure you'd be okay here alone for a little while."

"That's considerate of you. I'll be fine. I can nurse my broken, angry heart whether you're here are not. And I have Emmie to keep me company."

Brenda shrugged. "Okay. I'll be back in a bit." She grabbed her purse and car keys and left.

Ten minutes later, there was a knock on the door. Had Brenda forgotten something? Megan opened the door, leaving the chain in place. "What did you forget?" Her eyes widened, shocked to see Chase standing there. She frowned. "I thought you were Brenda."

"Yeah, I got that," he said with a halfhearted smile.

"I have nothing to say to you. You wasted your time coming all the way down here. The fact that I haven't returned your calls or texts should have been a clue. Goodbye." She tried to close the door in his face, but he stuck his foot in to block it.

"Megan, may I please come in? We need to talk."

If it had been anyone other than Chase, she'd be dialing 911.

"No, we don't. There is nothing you can say that I will believe."

"Please, Megan."

Shit. How could she say no to that face? That is why she left Lucky—she was too weak to withstand him. "Sure. But Brenda's not here."

He frowned. "You don't actually think I flew down here to see Brenda, do you?"

"It doesn't matter. Like I said, I have nothing to say to you. You might as well go home." But even as she said it, she unlatched the chain and opened the door.

"Sorry, I have some things I need to say to you. Will you sit down and at least listen?"

Megan folded her hands across her middle. She was about to sit on the sofa when she caught her reflection in the mirror. Thank God she'd showered, but she still wasn't at her best.

Oh, who cares? It's not like you're trying to impress him.

She plopped down onto the sofa. "Go ahead, I'm listening." She waved her hand as if commanding him to do so. Emmie jumped up next to her.

"Hey there, monster kitty." He patted Emmie on the head as he sat on the opposite side of the cat. "Please, just hear me out. First, I need you to know why I never told you that your mother sent me. I suspected it would be a big deal for you since you've always had an issue with your mom interfering in your life.

"I should have come clean from the start. But you were so disappointed after the contest, and we were drinking. One thing led to another. By the time we ended up in bed, I didn't want to say or do anything to spoil our time together."

He looked down and wiped his hands on his thighs. When he lifted his head, he looked her in the eye. "That's not completely accurate."

"You mean honest?" she interrupted.

He sighed deeply and stared at her. "May I continue?"

"Whatever," she said flippantly.

"I kept my mouth shut because I was crazy about you, and I knew you'd blow up. And I wanted to spend time with you that night. I wanted to be with you. For me, it was more than a drunken pickup. I need you to know that. I jumped at the chance to go to Vegas when your mom mentioned it."

She didn't know what to say. That sort of deflated the air in her balloon of anger.

"What about the next day?"

"Same reason, I suppose. But really, I was more concerned about the fact that we had gotten married. I was wrong not to tell you about the wedding. It was a mistake that I regret." He took her hands in his. "I'm sorry I hurt you. It was never my intention."

He stood and walked over to the hall table, picking up a couple of envelopes she hadn't noticed when he first came into the apartment. He offered them to her. "They're numbered one and two."

"I see that. Am I supposed to open them in that order?"

He nodded.

She shrugged. The sooner they got this over, the sooner he'd leave. She opened the envelope marked one. It held their divorce papers. He'd signed them.

A sharp pain stabbed her heart. She inhaled deeply. It wasn't as if she didn't know there were divorce papers. They'd talked about annulment or divorce off and on, but it had always been in the abstract. Nothing firm. It was also before they'd grown so close. She hadn't realized the utter defeat she'd feel.

Finally, she nodded, cleared her throat, and said, "Fine. Thank you for this. I'll get it to my attorney." She couldn't look at him. "Thank you." She had to get him out of here. She began to stand, but he held her in place.

"Open the second envelope."

She shook her head. "No, I will later."

"Now. Megan, I need you to open it now."

"Oh, all right." She unfolded a paper to find it was an application for a marriage license. She didn't understand. This made no sense. "What is this?"

"What does it look like?"

"I don't know."

He slid off the sofa, onto one knee beside her. He took her hands and brought them up to his heart. "I'm sorry that I hurt you. Please forgive me. I love you with all my heart. I want to marry you again. And this time, you will remember every detail. You're the most important person in my life. I need you. And I think you need me. We're good together. If I need to move down here to make you happy, I will."

She brushed a tear off her cheek. "You'd move to Nashville? For me?"

"Babe, I'd move to the moon to be with you. If it makes you happy."

Megan pulled a hand away and placed it over her own heart. "You're too much."

He cocked his head. "Too much? I hope that's a good thing." He gave her one of his sexy grins.

"I know there's a lot to work out. I can check into openings for firefighters in the area. Or if not, I can always do construction." He shrugged.

He'd give up being a firefighter for her. Another tear trickled down her cheek. Damn him for making her cry, even if these were happy tears. She swiped them away. She forgave him.

Before she could tell him, he pulled out a small jewelry box, and she gasped.

He opened the box to reveal a delicate silver shining star pendant. "You're my lucky star, Megan. Marry me. Again."

Her heart swelled with love for this man. She slid off the sofa, kneeled facing him. She placed her hands on his cheeks and kissed his mouth. "Yes, I love you, and I'll marry you. Again." She laughed. "Although I never signed those divorce papers, so we're still technically married."

"But this time I want to do it right. In front of our family and friends. And I want you to remember every minute."

"Sounds perfect."

"I want you to pick out your ring. So I waited. We can look here. Obviously, there are more options than back home." He kissed her again.

She shook her head, scrambling off the floor, pulling him up with her to the sofa.

"Chase, I've had a lot of time to think since I got back to Nashville. That's all I've done." She rolled her eyes. "It means so much that you would give up your life in Lucky for me." She squeezed his hand. "But I want to move to Lucky. Make our life there. I can write music anywhere. I can set up a recording studio or come down to Nashville once a month. We'll make it work."

Chase's eyes widened. "I can't believe you would trade Nashville for Lucky."

"As long as we are together."

Chase relaxed, content to hold Megan for the rest of their lives. They were lying on the sofa wrapped in each other's arms, keeping it PG 13, since Brenda could return from her errands at any time.

But he ached for Megan.

He stroked his finger idly along her arm. Listened to her happy chatter about all she'd need to do to prepare to move north.

"There is only one thing I'm disappointed about." His hand froze.

"I can't believe I let Espresso Yourself go. I wasn't going to, but when Bruce contacted me about a buyer with an offer too good to pass up, I said yes. It was impetuous and stupid of me. I should have waited. Thought about it more. Sometimes I let my temper get the best of me—or maybe I should say the worst."

"Really? I hadn't noticed."

"Oh, you." She pinched him in the side.

"Ouch."

"I'll have to keep an eye out for another property to start fresh."

He smiled, chuckling.

"What's so funny?"

"It's not funny. But I hope it's a nice surprise." She frowned. "Now I'm really curious."

"Hold on a sec," he said as he stood, and took another envelope out of his back pocket and handed it to her.

She pushed herself to a more upright position. "Another surprise?"

"Open it and see."

She opened it and pulled out a property deed. "Oh my God," she exclaimed.

"You don't have to start over, unless you want to, of course. I was the one who contacted Bruce. Espresso Yourself is still yours."

"Oh my, this is incredible. Thank you, Chase."

He nodded. "I hope it's okay. I couldn't let that place go. I guess I was hoping you'd change your mind. It broke my heart after all your time and hard work.

"I can't believe you did this for me."

"You're not mad that I did it without you knowing about it?" he asked, warily.

"Then it wouldn't be much of a surprise. Thank you." Her tears were threatening again.

"You're welcome." He sighed, and a smile broke out on his face. "We're lucky."

"Yes, we are."

Epilogue

Six months later

Lucky, Ohio

Megan Howard woke with a smile on her face.

Her fiancé, Chase, still slept soundly next to her. Who could blame him after his hectic forty-eight-hour shift ended yesterday? She gently stroked his sexy morning stubble.

She wished she could snuggle up to his heat on this chilly morning, but Brady was stirring and would need to go out. She scooted out of bed, throwing on her robe. As she tiptoed out of the bedroom, Emmie darted in and jumped up on the bed.

Megan stifled her laugh. Instead of the cat pouncing on Chase, she crawled onto Megan's vacated pillow and snuggled up to the back of Chase's head. She'd finally accepted Chase. No more surprise attacks.

Megan headed to the kitchen to start coffee. They had a lot to do before leaving that afternoon. She'd been invited to sing at a benefit at the Grand Ole Opry on Saturday night. She'd be singing her second single, "Lucky Star." It hit the country music charts at number forty-three and was climbing.

She sat at the kitchen table, making a list of what she didn't want to forget.

"Hey, there."

She gasped as her hand flew to her heart. "Oh my God, Kell, you almost gave me a heart attack. Ever heard of knocking?"

"Sorry," he said, grinning, holding up the key Chase had given him.

"No, you're not. You love scaring me just like you did when we were kids, only now you're an expert at stealth mode."

At least he had the decency to look chagrined. "Maybe just a little."

"What are you doing here so early? Why aren't you home packing?" Kell, Mom, and Mom's latest squeeze were coming with them to attend the show.

They'd decided to stop in Cincinnati to have dinner with Johnny Martin. Kell and Chase hadn't seen their friend in some time, and this was a great chance for a mini reunion.

"That's why I'm here. I can't go. You'll have to give my regards to Johnny. Maybe next time."

She glared at her big brother. "Why not? What's going on?"

"I got a job."

"What?" she squealed. "Does this mean you're sticking around Lucky?"

He nodded. "Looks like it. For now, anyway."

She stood and hugged her big brother. "What's the job?"

"Mayor Hendricks offered me the sheriff job. They were in a jam after Ted Andrew's heart attack and early retirement. It's a temporary placement until the next election. But I'll take it. I need to stay behind, get started on the job. The deputies are young. There's been a slew of break-ins that have the town council on edge. The mayor seems to think I have the skill set for the job."

"By *skill set*, do you mean since you know how to shoot a gun?"

He tilted his head and gave her a wicked grin. "Guess so."

"Congratulations. I'm so happy you'll be sticking around."

"Hey, what's up?" Chase asked as he strolled into the kitchen and made a beeline to the coffeemaker, hesitating to kiss Megan on top of her head. "You know, bro, you might want to call ahead—you never know when you might interrupt something." He gave Kell a penetrating stare, then winked at Megan.

Megan felt her face heat.

"Oh, thanks for that image. Geesh, she's still my little sister." Kell shivered.

Chase chuckled. "You're lucky I pulled on a pair of shorts and Megan has a robe on."

"Okay, okay. You made your point. I'll call next time."

"Kell has some news," she said.

Chase cocked his head. "Oh?"

"You're looking at the new sheriff of Lucky."

"No shit? That's awesome. Congratulations." He shook Kell's hand. "I was hoping you'd find a reason to stick around."

"Someone needs to keep you in line," Kell said with a smile.

The two men looked over at Megan at the kitchen table. She had a huge smile on her face.

"What?" Chase and Kell asked at the same time.

Megan stood and walked over to join them. "I'm so happy to have my two favorite men here, in my life. I couldn't be luckier."

"Amen to that." Chase said, slapping Kell on the shoulder.

Acknowledgements

There are so many people who encouraged and helped me along the way. I'm very pleased I finally have an acknowledgment page to thank them publicly.

A big thank you to Roxanne St. Claire, Lori Wilde, and Kristan Higgins, who each listened to my ideas and encouraged me at the very beginning. You'll never know how much I appreciated your time. It meant so much to me. Every new writer should be so lucky! I hope I wasn't too much of a "fan girl."

I must thank Romance Writers of America (RWA). Through my membership with them, I could join local and online groups.

My two local groups are Mid-Michigan Romance Writers of America (now known as Michigan Romance Writers) and Greater Detroit Romance Writers. Each group has connected me with other writers who have always been supportive in so many ways. A special thank you goes to my weekly writing buddies: Dawn Bartley, Lenore English, Patricia Kiyono, Lucy Kubash, Betty Meyette, Deb Moser, and Diana Stout.

I also want to thank the three Beta readers, Alby Blazo, Linda Fletcher, and Betty Meyette. I value your wisdom and writing expertise more than I can say.

Thank you to my editor Julie Sturgeon, CEOEditor, Inc. and my cover designer RCMatthewsArtist.

A huge shout out to Diana Stout, who spent many hours teaching me about formatting my book for KDP and troubleshooting my website.

My acknowledgments would be incomplete if I didn't recognize and thank my parents, Gerhard and Anne Klouman. They are no longer with us. But I am confident they are looking down with pride and joy.

Thank you to my family and friends who believed in me and encouraged me to keep writing, especially my children Elizabeth and Andrew and my husband Jeff. Your love and support over the years means everything to me.

Finally, thank you for reading this book. I sincerely hope you enjoyed Chase and Megan's story.

About the author

When I decided I wanted to write books, I knew the stories had to be like the ones I love to read, the kind with a happily ever after. It has taken several years, while I worked and raised a family, but now I am finally writing full-time.

I grew up in Ohio but have lived in Michigan for over thirty-five years where my husband and I raised our two children. The children are now adults and out on their own. We are living the dream as empty nesters, although we share our home with a rambunctious rescue dog named Brodie.

Five random things I like. ~ Listening to audiobooks while doing jigsaw puzzles. ~ Watching big screen rom-coms with a bucket of buttered popcorn. ~ Swimming ~ Indulging my craving for chocolate as often as I can. ~ A book, on a beach, with an umbrella cocktail.

Five random things I don't like. ~ Rude drivers ~ Finding my favorite pen, key fob, passport, shoes, slippers, etc. chewed by the above-mentioned rambunctious dog. ~ Cold weather ~ Seafood ~ Sweat inducing exercise.

If you would be so kind as to leave a review on Amazon.com or Goodreads, I would appreciate it. A review can be as simple as a comment and it will help other readers find my books.

To receive the latest news and surprises, be sure to sign up for my newsletter on my website: www.authorannestone.com.

Look for Lucky Break

Welcome to Lucky, a small town where anything is possible, and second chances really do come true.

What happens when a war-stricken former Marine gives up on finding true happiness because he thinks he's unworthy, meets the perfect woman — a single mom?

Can a woman whose ex-husband was a habitual cheater trust her heart or her child to a man who has made it clear he's not interested in forever?

Kell Howard expects his new job as sheriff to be peaceful—the opposite from his four tours as a marine. Instead, he needs to keep his PTSD hidden, while he solves a slew of burglaries and tries to avoid his mom's outlandish matchmaking ploys.

Dr. Becca James spends her time with her patients and raising her daughter. She's not ready to trust another man.

Neither Kell nor Becca is interested in dating, but they strike a mutually beneficial deal. In exchange for his help with major remodeling of her fixer-upper, she agrees to be his pretend girlfriend just long enough to get his mom off his back.

But, as their relationship deepens, they discover a secret that can destroy the trust they have been building.